Leah's Story

Leah's Story

by
C.M. Huddleston

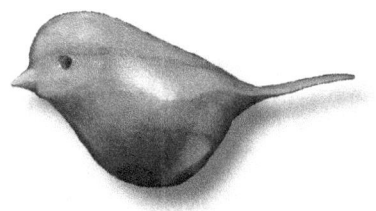

2017

Leah's Story

Published by:
Interpreting Time's Past Press
Text copyright © 2017 by C.M. Huddleston
Second Edition 2021

Text design by Interpreting Time's Past Press
Cover by Interpreting Time's Past Press
Cover scenic photograph by C.M. Huddleston
Cover bird image courtesy of Susan Benton of
Cedar Lake, Canada

ISBN-13: 978-0-9964304-5-6
Library of Congress: 2021916134
Names: Huddleston, C. M., author.
Title: Leah's story / C.M. Huddleston.
Description: 2nd edition. | Crab Orchard, KY: Interpreting Time's Past Press, 2021.
Identifiers: LCCN: 2021916134 | ISBN: 978-0-9964304-5-6 (paperback) | 978-0-9964304-6-3 (ebook)
Subjects: LCSH African Americans--Fiction. | African American women--Fiction. | United States--History--1815-1861--Fiction. | Slavery--Fiction. | Historical fiction. | BISAC FICTION / African American & Black / Historical | FICTION / African American & Black / Women | FICTION / Historical / Civil War Era
Classification: PS3608 .U32 L43 2021 | DDC 813.6--dc23

Study the past if you
would define the future.
Confucius

Oh, yes the past can hurt.
But the way I see it,
you can either run from it.
Or learn from it.

Rafiki in "The Lion King"

Leah's Story

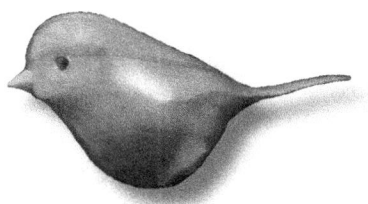

Explanation

Early summer heated the room to an uncomfortable degree the day I found this narrative in a small wood and leather traveling trunk hidden in a back corner of our house museum's attic. Old, musty smelling, yellowed typewritten pages, tied with now almost-rotted string and dated 1903, lay in the bottom of the trunk under several wrinkled, silk and cotton 1920s style dresses. Alongside, swaddled in tissue paper—which disintegrated when I picked it up—I uncovered a small, intricately-carved wood box. On the top, hewn animals and birds dotted a riverside landscape, each seeming to be alive, ready to take flight or simply walk off the edge. Slowly, so carefully, I rotated the box in my hands. On one end, I beheld a forest clearing where a small boy fished in a wide river; you could see the details in his cane pole. On the opposite end, a small Negro baby lay swaddled in a blanket, eyes closed as if in sleep. On the front, I gazed upon a plank dogtrot style cabin, standing on eight brick piers. A Negro man sat on the stoop next to a small girl, both whittled. As I opened the top, I saw the word *Leah* carved inside the lid, surrounded by all sorts of birds.

I laid it aside, still holding it in my thoughts as I examined the vintage clothing wondering how we could display the dresses as a special exhibit. Wanting a story to accompany the exhibit, I returned to the manuscript and read, looking for the owner's name and perhaps a clue as to how the trunk had remained unnoticed in the attic all these years. Finding neither an owner's name nor a reason for its presence, I now wish to pass along *Leah's Story*. Perhaps someone who reads these words will reveal the identity of Miss Elliott. I think the reason she wrote down these words will become evident.

C.M. Huddleston

Leah's Story
as told in
her own words
and written down
by S.B. Elliott

The Year 1827

I remember. The sun broke softly through the river's haze, rising and moving silently toward me over the rice fields as I picked my way across the swept dirt clearing between the cabin nearest the big house and those of the field slaves set somewhat apart. Warm tears ran down my cheeks and onto my neck, catching in my kerchief, caught before they reached the top of the colorless osnaburg shift I wore. My head drooped revealing the top of my black curly hair, full of dust and tangled beyond belief. My feet shuffled with each step, dirt stirring quietly around like the buzzing gnats always present there along the Georgia coast. I gave no thought to where I went. I simply walked toward someone who might give comfort. Someone who could ease my breaking heart.

My tears flowed not only for me, but for my Maum and Daddy I left behind, deathly sick in their bed in the little cabin near the house. Senator Elliott's words still rang in my ears.

"Little Leah, you go along now, out to the field slave cabins and don't you come back. You find a place to stay where the dysentery has not reached. Go find Daddy William. He'll take care of you. Don't come back. I'll take care of Maum Bess and Daddy Isaiah. You know I will, but don't you come back . . . hear child?"

He had been on his knees, right at my level. Face-to-face we was, as I begged to him to let me stay. He held me as the tears began to pool in my eyes, just as I had seen him hold his own little Susan. Yet, he sent me away. I knew my Maum was truly ill for she had not gone to the kitchen for three days now. Someone else cooked for Senator Elliott. Not that the man had eaten much. He had not taken much rest either, although Maum Grace had urged him to take care of himself. I had watched him move from cabin to cabin giving comfort and aid for some eighteen days now. Carrying water from the well. Carrying food for those still able to eat. And carrying off the dead.

Senator Elliott and Daddy William had toted each sheeting-wrapped body out cabin door after cabin door and placed them gently on a wagon pulled by the ol' plantation's strongest mule. Sometimes there lay only one. Other mornings, the dead piled high on the wagon bed. Looked like they might tumble right off the sides and into the dirt where the wagon stood. Tenderly, Daddy William drove those bodies up the road, out of sight into the longleaf pine forest where stood our little cemetery. I guess others dug those graves, for Daddy William never stayed gone for long. Some of our women marched resolutely up the path each night, holding smoking torches, into that dark forest and prayed over those graves. Some could barely walk for their grief and their tears. Old Maum Dinah always limped along, using her cane, mumbling in an old-country language I never knew and few remembered. Some said she helped the dead move on to a better place by saying the old words. Others sang the hymns, softly crooning "I looked over Jordan an' what did I see, comin' fo' to carry me home, a band of angels comin' after me, comin' fo' to carry me home." Mostly we mourned as more and more passed on to the glory land. Just so, just so.

Like he said to do, I found Daddy William. Hugging his tall legs, I shed more tears as he patted my back and whispered, "Hush, little Leah, hush child. Daddy William goin-a take care of you till your Maum's better. Now come along."

I dried my tears the best I could. Guess I was only about seven years old the day my Maum and Daddy left this earth. I listened to the words of Senator Elliott, and I never went back to that little cabin near the back door of the plantation house. I never kissed my Maum and Daddy goodbye. Never saw their smiling faces again. Never heard them whisper to each other in the night. Never saw my Daddy struggle to read the written word of his Bible. Never beheld my mother's hands as she wiped my face, tidied my hair, and sent me off to do my chores.

All day, I moved from chore to chore, cleaning, dusting, carrying firewood and water to the big house. Maum Grace fed me and made sure I ate. She made me rest in the heat of that July afternoon, on the pallet right next to the Senator's bed. I think I lay drowsy most of the late day and into dusk, having slept little the night before. That's where I was when Daddy William helped the Senator into the room and into bed. Poor, tired man, exhausted from days without enough sleep and worrying after all us slave folks. He never rose again on his own.

Next morning, Daddy William sent Phileas into Savannah, forty miles on horseback he rode to tell Mistress Martha her husband done took the dysentery. Later, they carried my Maum and Daddy out to the wagon. I stood and watched, Maum Grace holdin' me back from running to them. I cried 'til I was sick, vomiting all over the back stoop. Daddy William worried I had caught the dysentery, but Maum Grace knew better.

"Child's sick with grief, done lost both her maum and her daddy, now you leave her be. I see she's taken care of whilst you care for the Senator."

Next thing I knew, Mistress Elliott came in the town carriage for the Senator. Insisted on taking him back to Savannah to see the doctors, she did. Daddy William wrapped him in one of those colorful quilts Mistress Elliott used on their bed and carried him quietly to the carriage, shaking his large black head as he went. Now Daddy William didn't hold with doctors. He always believed prayer to our Lord could cure most any illness. Said if not, then the good Lord didn't want it to be.

But Mistress Elliott demanded the Senator be taken into town and like always, she got what she wanted. Senator often said she "was a force to behold." I guess he was right. She surely was that day. Just so, just so.

After getting the Senator settled, Daddy William shooed the carriage driver off the seat, lifted me up in his place, and climbed aboard. Now Mistress Elliott came out of the house holding a basket from Maum Grace and spied me sitting on the carriage's high seat. She looked at Daddy William the briefest of glances before asking, "Now Daddy William, what is Leah doing sitting up there?"

"She be going with us Mistress Martha. She my daughter now. Bess and Isaiah died and left her to my care. Where I go she goes. Where the Senator goes I go. So she goes. Just so, just so." His voice rang clear and sharp. Not demanding, purely stating fact. He never looked at Mistress Martha, sat there staring straight ahead, toward Savannah.

And so I went to Savannah. Now I had never, in all my seven years, left Senator Elliott's Laurel View Plantation. So as Daddy William drove toward Savannah, I gawked at all we passed, the quiet rivers with ships and barges filled with timber, livestock, and corn, and the slaves working field after field, some flooded fields of rice and others standing green in cotton. Oh, and the little villages of white people. More white people than I ever had seen.

As we drew nearer and nearer to Savannah, I saw houses like I had never even imagined. Two and three story houses with windows gleaming in the late day sun, many painted bright colors like pink, green, and even blue that near to matched the sky. I saw black carriages with glass windows pulled by as many as four horses, all of the same color with gleaming brass and polished leather harnesses. I saw black folks like me dressed in osnaburg and checked cottons, others dressed up in white people's clothes, black men in frock coats and their women in straw bonnets. Daddy William said they be house slaves or free coloreds. I'd never even heard of such a thing as free coloreds. But then and there, I decided if I could walk along proud like that, dressed like white folk, that I wanted to be one of those free coloreds.

In Savannah, all of us, black and white, being hot, thirsty, and tired, wearied as the carriage moved at a snail's pace along the river toward the Senator's home. Horses, wagons, hand carts, and carriages packed the broad avenues and filled the air with noise and dust. Smells of fish, dung, and garbage assaulted us. Although the town's live oaks shadowed each passageway, the air grew hotter and hotter. I thought I would suffocate. Daddy William unfailingly drove on, loudly urging carts and wagons out of his way. When I thought I could take no more, he turned into a shaded lane behind some large houses and stopped the carriage.

"Mistress Martha, we be home. Let me carry the Senator, and you lead the way to where you want him," stated Daddy William as he opened the carriage door to help Mistress Elliott alight.

How he carried the man, I don't know, for the Senator was not a small man. But carry him he did, into the house and into the master's bedroom, placing him ever so gently on the bed. Then he came back for me.

"Little Leah, this is Maum Charlotte. She will see to you," he stated as he guided me into the kitchen, his hand resting softly on my shoulder.

Again, I stood, deserted to the care of strangers, on my own. Charlotte ushered me to a stool, gave me warm corn muffins with fresh butter and a glass of cold milk. She talked on and on about my parents, how nice they were, how long she had known them, and asked about many others on the plantation. Finally, my voice whispered, "Twenty done died of the dysentery. My Maum and Daddy died. Is the Senator going to die? Will Daddy William keep me? What's going to happen to me?" I cried and cried, the tears making streaks down through the dust covering me from head to toe.

For ten days, I slept in Maum Charlotte's room next to the kitchen. I helped her daughters, Nancy and Rebecca, with the house chores. Daddy William came to see me each day. Held me in his lap and crooned quiet hymns in his deep bass voice. On the tenth day, the Senator died.

Poor Mistress Martha, there she sat beside the bed holding the Senator's hand, left alone with the Senator's two unmarried daughters from his first marriage, Miss Jane and Miss Corinne, and four children from their nine-year marriage. I knew Miss Susan as she was about my age, then came Miss Georgia only 'bout five. Finally, the little boys, Charles, age three, and the baby, Daniel. Of course, she had a house full of slaves and nursemaids to help her along. And Major Bulloch and Hester, his wife the Senator's older daughter, came right over to help out. Mistress Martha changed her dress to the blackest black while Rebecca and I helped the girls change to somber dark colors. I wondered why I could not have black to mourn my parents.

But death had not been satisfied by taking the Senator, for only a few days later little Charles took sick. I guess it was the dysentery. He lay ill for almost a month before death carried him out the door. Oh, how his black nursemaid and we did wail. But no louder than Mistress Martha. Again, I thought a heart would break into too many pieces to be repaired. I overheard Maum Charlotte tell Daddy William how Mistress Martha had already lost one son. Seems death never dwelt far away, for white folks or black folks. Just so, just so.

I never went back to Laurel View. I never saw my parent's graves. I lived in Savannah with Daddy William. I remember.

The Year 1829

I remember. It had not been quite two years since I left Liberty County and Laurel View. Mistress Martha, now she went back many times, took all those children too. They traveled to Charleston and to the North many times as well. Not me, I stayed right there in Savannah with Daddy William. He was my daddy by then, always will be. I barely remembers Bess and Isaiah.

I lived and worked there in Mistress Martha's big town house. Whoa was it big—three full stories with an attic. Now, it had a kitchen down in the basement and a big carriage house out back. Daddy William and I lived in one of the rooms over the carriage house. During the day, I cleaned, toted, and helped with the younger children. That little Daniel, oh he was so bright. He sang like an angel and drew beautiful pictures. A person could tell what the animal was when he finished drawing. I loved that little boy. Mistress Martha done spoiled him something terrible. So did his sisters.

I think it was because he was Master Elliott's only
surviving son.

Daddy William now lived all the time at Mistress
Martha's townhouse. Soon she let him bring his tools
from the plantation and set up a shop in one of Major
Bulloch's buildings down on the river front. Each day,
when my mornin' chores were finished, I took a basket
of food to the shop to feed Daddy William and the other
Negro workers. Sometimes there was only William and
Luke, his helper. Other days there might be three or
four more men helping Daddy William.

You see, Daddy William was a carpenter. He
built the most beautiful furniture you could ever ask for.
Each piece felt like butter where he planed the wood,
rubbing it so smooth. He could turn a lathe and shape
beautiful table legs or chair legs. He built from oak
and cypress and even pine. Sometimes, rich white men
would bring in maple or cherry or apple wood for Daddy
William and commission a special piece of furniture.
When I arrived each day, Daddy William would take
his work break, sit down, drink his buttermilk, and eat
whatever Maum Charlotte had packed. While he sat,
I measured, planed, cut, sanded, and learned. Using
leftover wood, I practiced turning the lathe by peddling
with my feet and holding the chisel just so. I was too
small at first to reach the lathe pedals while sitting on
the stool, so Daddy William made a pair of extensions

I could strap on over my bare feet. I practiced over and over, until I had four little table legs.

He would say, "Little Leah, now rub the sand with the grain of the wood and keep it dry, it'll work better" or "Leah, did you measure carefully? If'n you cut wrong it won't make a good table, things'll slide off the low side. Just so, just so."

Now Major Bulloch set aside part of the money Daddy William earned from making furniture. The rest he gave to Mistress Martha. He said he invested the set-aside money for Daddy William. Daddy William saved to buy his freedom and my freedom. He needed a heap of money, for Daddy William was a valuable slave. Carpenters brought a goodly sum on the market block. But, sometimes, Daddy William would ask the Major for a sum of his money for some small thing he wanted to buy. I remember one such day.

The Major's factoring business sat right next door to Daddy William's workshop, and Daddy William and I walked over after lunch and asked respectfully to see the Major.

"Major, I done needs a bit of my money. This here be Leah's birthday. She be nine years old this day. I think she done need a new dress and a bonnet, and shoes tha' fit. Don't you think she do? Why, look at the child, dressed how she is. She a disgrace to Mistress Martha. Don't you think so? I done declare, I got money, and I want to see her look respectful. Now if you could see fit to hand me a bit of that *vested* money, I'll see she done look nice. She'll make you proud."

Now I knew what Daddy William be up to. Daddy William always said, make the white folks think you is doing something to benefit them and they'll do what you wanted them to do in the first place. Just so, just so.

I purely stood beside Daddy William and kept quiet like he told me to do.

"Daddy William, there is no need for you to spend your invested money on little Leah. I think she has earned a new set of clothes, especially since this is her birthday," replied the Major.

Now, I had no idea and neither did Daddy William what day my birthday was. I did know I was born in the early spring and on my birthday the trees had begun to bud out and a warm breeze would blow across the way, followed by one that told ol' man winter still hung nearby barely out of sight. But from that day forward, March 26 stood as my birthday.

Major Bulloch took my hand and as Daddy William led the way. We walked up to Mister Low's big mercantile, and we walked right in the front door, like we belonged, being as we were with the Major. Before I knew what was happening, I had a new printed cotton dress, underthings, a cloth bonnet, and shoes no one else had ever worn. Daddy William approved of Major Bulloch's choices on all things 'ceptin' the dress. The

Major wanted pink, but Daddy William chose red. He knew red was my favorite color. There were not a lot of dresses to choose from, but we got one a bit big so I could wear it longer. Then the Major, he done turned to Mister Low's man and said to put it all on his account. He signed the big black ledger book while the other employee wrapped all my new things in brown paper and tied the bundle with string.

Daddy William asked, "Major, how do I pay the clerk man for these things?"

"Never you mind, William, it's taken care of."

When the Major left us at the door of the workshop, Daddy William said, "Now you run along back to Mistress Martha's and do your chores. Don't forget the basket, and when she asks about the package, you tell her it's your birthday, and I bought you a few things."

"But, Daddy William, the Major done paid for my new clothes. I can't lie to Mistress Martha."

"Oh, child, you not be lying. I worked for tha' ol' money the Major done spent. It t'were my money all right, it simply passed through the Major's pocket on the way to you." He patted my head as I left, then turned back to his work. I remember.

The Year 1832

I remember, yes I sure does remember. Now woodworking was not all I learned. Miss Susan and Miss Georgia had a nursemaid, and they climbed up to the classroom on the third floor each morning and practiced their letters and numbers. I learned my letters and numbers by cleaning close by to the door and listening as the nursemaid taught the Senator's daughters. Sometimes I snuck their books off and tried to read. Now Miss Susan figured out real quick what I was about. She told Mistress Martha on me. I figured I was in trouble and would be sent away.

"Leah, if you want to learn to read and write, ask permission. Don't go sneaking Susan's books. Take this book and tablet and sit quietly each day during class. You can take a break from chores to learn," Mistress Martha instructed as she handed me a tablet to write on and a book. Now the book looked like many a child had used it to learn to read, but the tablet was new, identical

to the ones her girls used. Soon others had to do my
chores while I went to the classroom.

Now don't think that nursemaid liked having a
darkie in the room learning to read and write. No, she
did not. But she'd heard Mistress Elliott and simply
kept on teaching. Ignored me every minute of every day.
Didn't matter to me a'tall. No, Daddy William and I
intended to be free coloreds some day, and me learning
to read and my numbers would help us along the way.

I learned all right. I could soon read my Daddy's
Bible 'ceptin' for those big names like Ebenezer. I had
to have help with those. I would ask Miss Susan or
Mistress Martha when I was stumped. I read to Daddy
William most every night until the darkness came to our
little room. Just so, just so.

Those were good years in Savannah. Mistress
Martha gave me Miss Susan's outgrowed clothes to
wear. I had such pretty dresses and even had shoes for
most days and shoes for Sundays. Mistress Martha
insisted on shoes for her house slaves. She even handed
me a straw bonnet with a blue ribbon for wearing to
church on Sunday. Other days I wore my cloth bonnet.
Maum Charlotte kept it clean and starched. We were
house slaves and needed to dress respectable.

Now let me tell you about Maum Charlotte. She
was what people call mulatto. She had a black Maum
and a white daddy, some slave owner. I never knew
who, but it was *not* the Senator. He didn't hold with

such things. Many slave owners did. Maum Charlotte's
skin was the color of biscuits coated in butter and then
baked. Her eyes were amber, not black like most of us
Negroes. She was a little thing, only about five feet two,
and carried herself like a queen she did. Always wore a
blue kerchief tied over her hair, 'ceptin' on Sundays. On
Sundays, she wore a blue patterned skirt and bodice,
with real lace on the sleeves and a blue hat of the finest
straw with flowers and a teeny, tiny bird in a nest. Off
to church she walked, every Sunday, head held high and
Daddy Luke trailing along behind. He might have been
her husband, but him being all black, she didn't see him
as her equal. No, no, Maum Charlotte was kind and
gentle, but she done knowed her place sat a bit higher
than all us.

On Sundays, Daddy William and I would drive
the Elliotts in the family's black carriage to the big
stone church where all the white people went. If the
weather was nice, sometimes they walked to church.
If they walked, Mistress Martha could show off her
new gown and all her children, all dressed in their
Sunday best. Daddy William walked with them on those
Sundays. Then we was free to go off to the little Negro
Baptist church for our own worship. He simply had to
be back to see them home after the service if they didn't
want to walk. If they walked, then Major Bulloch and
Mistress Hester would see them home.

I still had work to do each day. Now, my work day was long, but not hard. I dusted, swept, carried water, toted firewood and ash, helped with the wash, and learned to iron. I cared for little Daniel when his nurse took her day off. I loved that little boy like a brother. I loved Miss Susan and Miss Georgia as well. I think they cared for me. Mistress Martha cared for all her house slaves. She made sure we had plenty to eat, clothes to wear, medicine when we were sick, and a soft clean place to sleep. Some people now days say slave masters were cruel. Don't get me wrong, Miss Elliott. Many were. I saw families split and sold to different masters; slaves whipped and starved and beaten. Not Mistress Martha. Never saw her raise a hand to one person, black or white. Major Bulloch and Mistress Hester carried on the same way. Major Bulloch even sponsored some free colored people.

You see in Georgia, if you was a free colored you needed a white person to act as your guardian. They made sure you paid your taxes and behaved. They helped you get positions or jobs and helped with your money. You could not have your own account at a store without a sponsor. Major Bulloch kept busy sponsoring colored people, sometimes three or more each year.

Now by 1832, Senator Elliott's daughter Hester Bulloch lay dead in the family crypt, and the Major and his son, little James, lived there with us. The Major, a quiet spoken man, well he grieved for his dead wife and helped Mistress Martha with the money matters. Back in the first part of 1829, Mistress Martha had also buried Miss Jane Elliott who had not been married long, maybe a year, to a Mister Law when she was burned in a house fire. Oh, such a pitiful thing she was, only lived a day or so after the fire. Her sister Miss Corinne cried and cried when Miss Jane died. Death seemed to follow Mistress Martha around looking for someone else to take.

Mistress Martha's father, ol' General Daniel Stewart, passed not long after Miss Jane. Him being a Revolutionary War hero, the church bells in Savannah rang and rang when his death was announced. Many, many people attended his funeral at the Midway Congregational Church. Daddy William drove the family in the carriage, like always, and stood outside the church door to listen. I didn't go. He told me all about the burying when he returned. The family stayed a few days at Cedar Grove Plantation, before coming back to town. Cedar Grove belonged to the ol' General and his wife Mistress Sarah, the General's third wife. She lived there until her death came not long after the General's. Just so, just so.

Daddy William brought home all the Laurel View plantation gossip. Who had married who, who had new babies, and how worried all the folks were about being sold. You see, Senator Elliott had planned to sell even before his death. A Mister Maxwell finally closed the deal and took over. Now the Senator never sold a slave unless he was selling one so as they could marry someone on another plantation. No one could figure what Mister Maxwell would do. Daddy William and I belonged to Mistress Martha, so we had no worries 'bout being sold from the plantation. Only Mistress Martha could sell us.

Now the Senator's death had made Mistress Martha a rich woman. Her father's death made her even richer than she had been before. Soon, I heard her exclaim how she had too much land and too many mouths to feed. I sure hoped she wasn't talking about Daddy William and me. Just so, just so.

Now, I need to go back and talk about the Major again. I don't rightly know why we always called him the Major. He wasn't in the army far as I knew. Some said he served in that there War back in the 18-teens. Guess they were right. He was a handsome man, I can tell you. He had a head of wavy dark hair, a soft mouth and smile, and eyes that betrayed his every thought. He also had a head for business. Didn't take with drinking or dueling. Went to church twice a week and loved Mistress Martha. And I don't mean like a step-son-in-law. I mean he loved her. You could read it in his face every time he saw her. He worshiped the woman. Gave her anything and everything she desired. I think Mistress Martha really desired the Major, if you know what I mean.

The Major worked as what they called a *factor*, buying and selling cotton, rice, lumber, and other such things, right here in Savannah for the early part of his life. He also helped people with legal matters such as probates, wills, and such. Don't think he was actually a lawyer, though his partner Mister Dunwody sure was. The Major was also a banker, a beat commander, and a member of a fine organization called the Chatham Artillery. Oh, and the Major did love his machines.

Why, he had in his office a machine what could make copies of any letter or document he wrote. Called it a Patent Portable Copy Machine, he did. I loved to visit his office and see the machines. Early on, not long after he married Mistress Hester, he invested in the Steamship *Savannah,* first steamship to cross the ocean. Him and Mistress Hester even met President James Monroe when he came to visit. Just so, just so.

They done traveled down the river with the President and all those dignitaries on that steamship. Banners flew and people cheered. At night the Senator and Mistress Martha, Major Bulloch and Mistress Hester dressed up in silk and such and went to a big tent for a party. Daddy William told me all 'bout the events here in Savannah. He said Savannah done herself up proud.

Now, when the Major and little James came to live with us, his wife Hester was very ill. She required nursing all day and all night. She was in great pain, and the doctors came and went day after day. Mistress Martha and the Major took turns sitting with her at night. Sometimes, Maum Charlotte sat up with her and let Mistress Martha sleep. Then Mistress Hester passed in February of 1831. The family had recently put away their black clothes from mourning the General and back out they came. Maum Charlotte and I ironed black dresses and petticoats for all the women and girls. The Major and little James wore black armbands.

Little James by that time been about eight years old. He attended school and was as smart as a whip. While his mother lay ill, Mistress Martha took over and made him part of her children. She treated him like one of her own, never the least bit like her step-grandson. The girls, Miss Corinne, Miss Susan, and Miss Georgia all called him "brother Jimmie." The Major tried to be a father to all Mistress Martha's children. Miss Susan and Miss Georgia took right to him. Not Miss Corinne, she being older remembered the Senator and seemed to resent the Major.

Now as 1831 progressed, I couldn't help but notice how the Major and Mistress Martha spent more and more time together. They talked quietly to one another in the evenings. Once or twice I caught them hugging real tight, and I thought at the time they might have been kissing. Mistress Martha looked so embarrassed. Now she was still a beautiful woman, always had been said Daddy William. He said that's why the Senator married such a young girl. Why, he was more than 20 years older than her. Even had a daughter older than her. But he fell in love and so did she. Toast of the town, the Senator and Mistress Martha.

But, I learned a thing or two in life, old love fades, then new love comes in strange ways. I watched as the widow Martha Stewart Elliott fell in love with the handsome widower James Stephens Bulloch. I kept their secret for many months. At least I thought I was the only one who knew. Everyone seemed surprised when they married in early May, when Savannah was at its prettiest. It was a quiet ceremony, only family and a few friends. Corinne didn't attend, but the other children stood by as their mother married a man they already considered their father. Corinne had married Mister Robert Hutchison, a very rich Scotsman, back in January of that same year. Seems to me she may have been off on her honeymoon when Mistress Martha married.

The talk began almost at once. Now in Savannah, each and every house had one or more house slave. They talked among themselves, over back fences, at the market, in the many town squares, and at their socials. They shared the bits of gossip overheard from their masters. They talked about who got married, who had affairs, who was expecting, who drank too much, and anything and everything else. The talk about Mistress Martha and the Major was not good. Everyone speculated how they could marry after living together for the last few years. I believe people expected them to go on acting like brother and sister for all their lives.

Well, in my mind and Daddy William's, their living in the same house was what created their love and made it so strong. Imagine them living together those years. Seeing each other each day. Seems to me that living and traveling together, caring for each other's children, and sharing such a past made them love each other even more. Probably also had something to do with how attractive each one was.

Now, I was twelve that year, same age as Miss Susan. We had whispered about how those two looked at each other, all lovey-dovey. Didn't surprise me none. Things changed when Mistress Martha done married the Major. I think it was the talk about town. Suddenly the family spent most time at General Stewart's old plantation, Cedar Grove. The General's wife had passed not long after he did, so the Major bought it for Mistress Martha using the Senator's money and part of her inheritance. They took trips to Charleston and visited relatives here and there. Daddy William sometimes drove them in the carriage, but most often Mistress Martha left him in charge here in Savannah. He continued to make furniture and when Miss Susan and Miss Georgia were away, I spent my days in the wood shop.

Daddy William encouraged me to work the wood. I could use any scraps I wanted as long as I had a plan. "Know what' youse going to come out with befor' youse begin," he always said. Soon I learned how to draw out what I wanted to build, small tables, lap desks, wooden boxes, candle holders, and all sorts of other objects. I realized I could see things in the wood. I could see what it could become and how it would look finished. As the years passed, Daddy William often sold pieces of my furniture and objects so I would have spending money. We didn't tell the Major or Mistress. You see, Daddy William and I still hoped to buy our freedom. We saved whatever we could. Cost a lot of money to buy freedom. We decided we would not buy freedom unless we could both buy freedom.

Now, Miss Elliott, don't take my words wrong. Daddy William and me, we was happy. We had good food each and every day and nice clean clothes. I could read and write, though Mistress Martha had suggested I not tell anyone 'ceptin' William I could. Most white people didn't hold with teaching coloreds to read and write. Figured it made them more likely to escape and go North.

But me and Daddy William, it's well . . . you see, we be'd afraid Mistress Martha might need to sell us, you know she had all those mouths to feed. Daddy William and I planned to open a furniture making shop if we ever got free. Other free colored folks down at the Negro Baptist church even offered to help us get settled when and if we could buy freedom. I remember.

The Year 1833

But as I said, things changed. Early the next year—let's see that would've been 1833—the Major's mother, Mistress Powell she was, having remarried after his father died young, done passed away, and him being the only remaining son, he had to take care of her estate. He already cared for his late brother John's two children, William and Jane.

That same year, Mistress Martha gave birth to Anna Louisa, a beautiful dark-haired tiny one. Oh! did things change so much. Major Bulloch carried that baby constantly when he was home. The other children teased him saying he would have carried her to his office if Mistress Martha had allowed. Totally besotted with her he was. Just so, just so.

Mistress Corinne and her husband, Mister Hutchison, came many afternoons to the house and spent the evening. Mistress Corinne, now she was a quiet, reserved young woman, always kind and pleasant to be around. Don't know how she stood being with Mister Hutchison, 'ceptin' he adored her. Worshiped the ground she walked on, he did. Had this terrible way about him—some said it was because he was a Scotsman. I had to ask Miss Susan what a *Scotsman* was, and she showed me how far away Scotland was on the classroom globe the Major had purchased for Master Jimmie. I still didn't know why being from Scotland explained Mister Hutchison's way of talking and saying things he might have better kept in his head.

Other things had changed. Miss Susan and Miss Georgia attended the Chatham Academy each day. Master Jimmie went as well. Most days, Daddy William had to drive them to and fro in the gig. So no more classes were held in the school room upstairs. But because the Major and Mistress Martha loved books there were many to be had in the house. Mistress Martha allowed me to read each and every one of those books. Mistress Martha took Miss Susan and Miss Georgia to the lending library where they had a subscription. They paid a fee to borrow books, you know. They brought home several books each week, so Mistress Martha allowed me to read them if my chores were finished. The Major, him being a factor, always brought home the latest newspapers and magazines. After all the family was finished reading them, Mistress Martha handed them to Maum Charlotte for wrapping things in the kitchen. At first I snuck them out when Maum wasn't paying me no mind.

One day, as I reached for a newspaper while passing through Maum Charlotte's kitchen, she whispered, "Leah, I leave them out for you each time on top of tha' barrel of flour. When you and Daddy William be done readin', lay it on top of the barrel of cornmeal, and I know you be done, child."

I also learned from Mistress Martha and the Major how to talk correctly. I heard them correct Miss Susan, Miss Georgia, and Master Daniel time and time again about their grammar. Never had to correct Master Jimmie—some said he was born an old man. So I listened and I learned. Now my grammar may not be as good as it should be, but I learned. I studied Jimmie's globe of the world and learned all the countries. I did arithmetic. Once I even carried off one of the Major's books on architecture—he was always learning something new—I loved the drawings of houses and furniture. I learned a valuable lesson that day. Don't ever take the book someone else is reading.

"Leah, Leah," the Major done called throughout the house.

"Yes, sir, I'm here," I answered.

"Leah, did you take my book on Classical architecture? I left it on the table beside my chair."

I hung my head and quietly answered, "Yes, sir."

"Well, Leah, I am reading that book. I need it now."

I quietly ran up the stairs to the classroom and promptly brought it back to the Major and handed it over without saying a word.

"Leah, never again take a book without asking. Do you understand, child?"

"Yes, sir, Major I do, I surely do," I replied without raising my head.

Never raised his voice nor his hand to me. He was truly a gentleman in my eyes. But I knew I had done wrong. I also knew that if I asked, any book would be loaned to me.

In February, we celebrated the 100th anniversary of the colony of Georgia. Now not much was done as some didn't want to remember the days of old King George's rule, but Savannah being the first settlement in the Colony did enjoy a small parade, and the family made toasts at a fancy dinner. Daddy William and I watched the parade from an upper window.

Daddy William bought me a pocket knife for my birthday that year. Not a usual gift for a 13-year-old girl, but I desired one so badly. You see, I had discovered whittling. Congo, one of Major Bulloch's slaves worked with Daddy William most days. Congo could see things in wood too. He could see small animals and birds. Then he would take a knife and make a thing come out so we could all see it. He smoothed the surface of each creature with bits of sand and rubbed other parts with strips of leather. Congo carried a small lion in his pocket, one he had carved out many years before. I read about lions in one of Master Jimmie's books. Congo swore he had seen lions before he came to America. I believed he had, for his little pocket carving looked exactly like the picture in Jimmie's book.

Congo showed me how to take off the parts of the wood that were hiding the animal or bird. First I worked with soft wood like pine or cypress. Later I learned to whittle the harder woods. Cut my thumb many a times, I did. I learned to use a chisel when I worked with large pieces of wood. I really liked working with driftwood, and Daddy William would take me down to the river's edge to look for pieces. Sometimes Congo went along. Oh, I remember, those was good days.

The Years
1834
to
1836

Now, often, most like every summer, Mistress Martha and the Major took those children and went off up North. Had to get away from Savannah's heat and disease. Malaria, yellow fever, cholera, all those sicknesses came each and every summer. Some years worse than others. So in the late Spring, off they would go to New York or Connecticut, stay all summer, and come home in the late Fall when Savannah got cooler and healthier. Went by steamboat, each time. Now this time, the Major insisted they go to Hartford, Connecticut, so Master Jimmie and Master Daniel could attend Isaac Webb's Academy, situated in a nearby town to Hartford. Talked about it all that winter, selling Mistress Martha on letting Daniel go to boarding school with James. I think the Major done invested in Mr. Webb's school. He talked about how much the boys would learn and how prepared they would be for their college studies.

The girls, Miss Susan and Miss Georgia,
attended a lady's academy along with Miss Matilda.
Now don't you ask me about Miss Matilda Bulloch, as
I can't rightly say who she was or how she was related to
the family. I only know she lived with us for some years.
Nice young woman, if I remember correctly, she died of
consumption, just so, just so.

Now while they was there, in Hartford, they
lived in a boarding house. Can you imagine, living in a
few rooms of a house full of strangers. Strangers. My oh
my. Miss Susan told me stories about taking meals in
a large dining room. One story always made us giggle.
She and Miss Georgia would scrunch up their eyes and
pretend to be mostly blind like Mister Montgomery who
lived there in the boarding house. Miss Georgia said
he made pig noises when he chewed. Also, Miss Susan
could talk like those Irish folks what lived up North, she
could make us all laugh and laugh. We had Irish down
here, like up North, but they was poor white trash, and
the family didn't associate with them none.

Now, we all expected them back in the Fall of
1834, but only the Major returned. Daddy William said
it was because Mistress Martha was increasing again.
Such a polite way to say she was going to have another
baby. The Major done come home several times during
the winter. And again the next winter. Mistress Martha
and Miss Susan wrote letters to me and Daddy William
now and again.

Now there is another story from those years you need to know, Miss Elliott. Mistress Martha took Maum Charlotte's daughter Nancy with her North. Nancy helped care for the little ones and served as Mistress Martha's lady's maid. Nancy could read and write, and she done sent letters to Maum Charlotte. Now Maum Charlotte never learned to read or write so I read those letters out loud when they came. I wrote back her replies. Mostly she told Nancy to do her work and that she loved her. It 'bout broke Maum Charlotte's heart when Nancy began writing about a free colored man she had met at church. Kept saying she done lost her baby.

Now Daddy William, he took sick in the summer of 1835, right about the time Mistress Martha done had her second baby girl, Miss Mittie, named for her mother Martha. Malaria, it was. Maum Charlotte and me thought he would pass him being so sick. Could not keep down even the slightest sip of water, and oh, how hot he was. We tried calling the doctor to the house, but with Mistress Martha and the Major being up North, Mistress Corinne now lived in the big house her father the Senator had built. She and Mister Hutchison was away up North that year. So us slaves had to suffer on our own.

Course the Major's uncle done checked in on us now and then. Made sure we was working and such. Strange now to think back on it. He lived right nearby, but we could have left at any time, gone North and been free. But we didn't. No, I guess we had a sense of responsibility to Mistress Martha and the Major. We knowed we was owned by them, but it was something more. Can't rightly tell you why but . . . well, we just didn't.

Now back to my story. Daddy William recovered from the malaria right as the family returned home. He had relapses several times over the next few years, but never as bad as that first time. He took to driving Major Bulloch as they settled all those estates the Major managed. Miss Susan and Miss Georgia stayed in the North and went to a lady's finishing academy. Master Jimmie and Master Daniel stayed at their school too. So, I had only little Anna and the baby to help with.

Maum Charlotte barely spoke for most of the next year. You see, Nancy didn't come home. She didn't really escape, she purely up and left Mistress Martha, and went off with people from the colored church up there in Hartford. They told her she was free. Now the Major was furious, only time I ever saw him so. He went to court to have her returned, but that judge up there said Nancy was free because the Major done took her to a free state. Mistress Martha declared to Maum Charlotte how Nancy could not take care of herself. Said she had no way to earn money or keep herself. So Maum Charlotte worried even more. It was a worrisome thing, it was.

Daddy William and me done talked about it, over and over with every letter from Nancy. Now you see, Nancy could read and write. Nancy dressed well and talked like a lady. She didn't marry the man she met at church, instead she found herself employment as a seamstress and lived with a free colored family. I know because I wrote Maum Charlotte's letters and read the ones Nancy sent back. Seemed to me, Nancy reckoned exactly what she was doing. Just so, just so.

The Year 1838

I remember. Can't never forget such a year. Mistress Martha and the Major changed that year. There came to the house a lot less laughter. The boys, Masters Daniel and Jimmie, was still in the North. The Major seemed lost. Mistress Martha cried often. The girls, Miss Susan and Miss Daisy, everyone called Miss Georgia, *Miss Daisy*, well, they came home for Christmas in 1837 and didn't go back to school. Things felt as though they was some how changing.

In the spring of 1838, we left Savannah for the colony of Roswell. Took us several weeks of travel to go so far. Mistress Martha, Miss Susan, Miss Daisy, and little Anna and Mittie rode in the carriage. We had three big wagons full of household goods. Pots and kettles, food stuffs, beds and mattresses, chairs, the old General's dining table, and all its chairs, china and glassware packed in straw. Clothes and bedclothes, trunks full of books, the table silver, everything you can imagine packed in those wagons and pulled by oxen or mules. Daddy William drove the carriage. I sat beside him every day, 'ceptin' when I walked.

The Major had done declared I was to stay in Savannah, but Daddy William stated softly but firmly, "Where I go, Leah goes."

Mistress Martha lowered her head at that, I think she was holdin' back a laugh, and said "James, we can't go without William, he won't go without Leah, so let the child go."

So I went.

Daddy Luke, Maum Charlotte, Daddy Stephen, Maum Rose, and Maum Grace went along. The first day of the trip, Major Bulloch had the carriage, horses, wagons, and all of us loaded on a sloop, and we headed up the river to Augusta. I'd never traveled on a boat before, but Daddy William placed his arm around me and promised I would like it. He also promised to keep nearby. So I sat on the deck, watched the shore slide by and whittled. I think I found my first seabird that day, inside a small piece of driftwood I found minutes before we walked up the gangplank.

Once we reached a small, dirty river town named Augusta and unloaded all the master's things, we met up with the horses and wagons what had gone on overland from Savannah. Then, the hard part of the journey began. As we moved farther north and west each day, the land became hilly and full of streams and

rivers to cross. At night we camped under canvas sheets.
I remember thinking Mistress Martha, so used to her
comforts would be miserable. Instead, she took to the
journey like a true pioneer. Often during the day she
walked alongside the carriage with Miss Susan and Miss
Georgia, despite her increasing again. Just so, just so.

We traveled for three weeks before we came to
the Chattahoochee River. A ferry man took us across
one wagon at a time. Took all day to ferry them wagons
and horses and us people across. First really hot day we
had. I spent my day wading in the shallows, watching
birds, and resting. First day we had not walked all day
from morning until night.

Directly across the river, Master Barrington
King waited on our arrival. As we progressed up the tall
hill on the other side of the river, I gawked at the pine
and hardwood forest surrounding the dirt lane. There
were trees everywhere, so packed together, seemed like
you could not walk among them, all the way up that hill.
At the top of the hill, a large brick building and some
smaller wood cabins were all there was of the *colony of
Roswell*. I could not believe the Major had brought his
family to the wilderness, a wild untamed wilderness, like
something out of a fairy tale. Next, Master Barrington
King led us to a large cabin built of nothing more than
logs stacked one on top of another. No glass in any of
the windows, only wood shutters to keep out the rain
and insects and snakes. It had rooms added here and

there on the cabin, where several families slept and ate, all together like. Mister Roswell King greeted the Major and Mistress Martha, like they was family. For the life of me, I could not figure out why we had traveled so far, to a place with so little.

Soon afterward, the Major moved us to a small farm with two log cabins. The family took the largest one, and us colored folks the other. We took up caring for the family, like we had for years back in Savannah. Mistress Martha gave birth to a strong boy not long afterward. They named him Charles.

The Major traveled back to Savannah and Liberty County and brought more slave families north. Daddy William went along and brought back his tools.

Now that's the year the Steamship *Pulaski* done blew up and sank. Seems everyone in Savannah knew someone who died. Mistress Martha lost her last stepdaughter. You see, Mister Hutchison, Mistress Corinne, and those two blonde-headed, little girls of theirs sailed on that ship. Left Savannah on the 13th of June it did. Now I remember hearing how the *Pulaski* stopped in Charleston and picked up more passengers, then out of sight of the coast about 11 at night after almost all was in bed, the boiler blew. That would have been the 14th. The ship burned and most of it sank. Mister Hutchison, well, he lived and ended up on a raft of debris with some others. Mistress Corinne and the youngest must have died during the night. But the next morning, little three-year-old Connie, they called her, been found with some other people on a raft that floated up. She spent the next day with Mister Hutchison and those survivors on the big raft.

Now they had some provisions what had floated by and more and more people made their way to the floating raft of debris. I can't likely remember how many days they floated, though I seem to remember it was five days. They endured rain and wind, thirst and burning sun. Years later, when the memory was not so fresh, Mister Hutchison done told Mistress Martha how little Connie begged for three cups of tea when they reached New York. He done broke down and cried, right then all those years later, while remembering how his child had suffered.

Then during a storm, Mister Hutchison with his daughter in his arms made for a safer place on the raft when he stepped on the tail of the cloak covering them both. Little Connie and the cloak flew into the billows as he stumbled. They said he barely spoke again until rescue came.

Over one hundred folks, white and colored, rich and simple working folk alike died on the *Pulaski*. Only 'bout fifty survived. I thought so often of Mister Hutchison's loss and how he could stand to go on livin'. Savannah and Charleston all mourned, seemed everyone, white or black, knew someone who perished. We had barely reached Roswell when the word came about the *Pulaski*. Those days was hard. Hard living, hard remembering. Still, I do remember.

The Year 1839

I remember. I first saw snow in 1839. No, not here in Savannah, in Roswell, where the Major chose a piece of hill top land near the cotton mill and began building a home. Daddy William and some of the colored men helped. Other white men started building houses in the colony, including Mister Roswell King. They built a little Presbyterian Church and a small school house. That first winter, when we all lived in the cabins, seems I stayed cold. Wrapped in blankets, we hauled water and did our chores. Next year, the Major made sure we all had coats and warm socks and shoes. Still, I stayed cold, that's one reason I came back to Savannah. To get warm, just so, just so.

Now, the next summer, Daddy William talked the Major into letting me work full time in the workshop. Oh, how I wanted it. I'd planned to ask the Major myself, but Daddy William, well, he had a better idea.

"Major," he started, "we done got so much work to do. You know I is helping build your new house, I is building furniture, I is building pews for the new church, I is helping with repairs at the mill, and I is even some days trying to get a bit of sleep. But Major, I is getting old. I purely too old to keep working this hard. Now you see, I want everything in your new house to be fine and elegant for Mistress Martha, has to be done right, you know it does. But, Major, I also need to eat and sleep and sometimes even go to the privy!"

"Now, William," the Major began. But before he could even finish.

"Major, I done thought of a' answer. You got too many house slaves while you is living in the cabin, and well, Leah is such a help in the workshop. You done seen her work. Now, let me have her help 'til the house is finished. Mistress Martha won't miss one girl helping out in the house, why she'll probably be happy to not have her underfoot."

Daddy William got ready to begin his next argument, but before he could even get started, Mistress Martha smiled and said, "James, allow her to go. Daddy William will talk himself hoarse with one reason after another until he is sick and needing some medicine. Better to take your loss while you're still ahead."

So I started working all the time in the workshop. Some days I worked on furniture. One day I turned stair railings. Another, I made stair treads. A

Mister Ball and his white workers from the North did most of the framing work on the house. The Major and him would look at a book about once a day and discuss how the trimming would be done. William and I kept working on the little things. I liked being in the workshop all day with Daddy William. Just so, just so.

Miss Elliott, I do have to brag a bit about my work. You see, the big ol' staircase in the front of the house done curved at the top. Daddy William and I had made all the trim work, the railing, the treads, and such. But one bit of trim done stumped us. You see, this piece of wood had to curve right around like and had to have scallops along the bottom edge to match all the others going up. It was thin wood, and Daddy William and I had made three of those pieces and each one had done broke in two as we tried to shape it into place. We done worried ourselves something terrible about how to make that piece.

Now, one morning real early, I went to the shop and picked up a piece of leather we was using as a pattern for the trim. I kept thinking about our situation when suddenly, I knew what to do. I took the leather pattern piece and cut another one, the exact width of the curved section, applied some stain, and ran to the house. I had to bend out over the staircase and put it just so, but it worked. I used some glue and placed the piece in between the other trim we had already applied. I used some small tacks to keep the edges in place while it dried. Then I sat back against the step, admired my work, and watched glue dry.

"Leah, what in heaven's name are you doing?" asked Major Bulloch, waking me from a sound sleep.

"Oh, Major, you done startled me. I's just watching glue dry and guess I fell asleep."

"Well. . . , I guess watching glue dry would make anyone fall asleep," he said with a chuckle. "But *why* are you watching glue dry, is the question?"

"Well, Major, I done solved the problem of this piece of trim what kept breaking each and every time Daddy William and me put it in this here curve," I told him smartly.

The Major walked directly below the problem spot, stared up, and just started laughing.

"Leather, you used leather. Leah, you are one smart girl. It looks exactly like the rest of the trim. Get a bit of shellac on it, and no one will ever know the difference," he stated.

"No, sir, Major, me and you, we'll know."

"I won't tell if you won't," the Major replied.

Of course, I told Daddy William, and I think the Major done bragged to one and all about how a girl had solved the problem of the curved trim. He made me proud telling that story. You see, the Major didn't tell how a *slave* girl had solved the problem. He always said *Leah* solved the problem. Like I was *someone*. I think that's when I realized I was someone. Not just a slave, but *someone* with a purpose.

Now I guess you are wondering what brought all those rich people to the wilderness. Why, Miss Elliott, it was the cotton mill brought them all there. Mister Roswell King and his son Master Barrington King started it, and then others done invested. Even the Major's sister Mistress John Dunwoody and her husband left their plantation and moved up north in Georgia. They settled right next door to the Major. Some families came to work at the mill, others came to work the land. They grew the cotton for the mill. Us colored folk, well, we came because we followed our masters wherever they went. Just so, just so.

I came to like Roswell. It became my home as Savannah had been before and Laurel View before Savannah. The summers weren't as hot as down on the coast. The river stayed clean and full of fish. The autumn brought bright reds and oranges to the trees. All kinds of birds sang. Deer and big ol' turkeys wandered the woods. Daddy Luke had a heavy ol' shotgun the Major gave him. He'd bring home rabbits and turkeys and possums for us to eat.

Now, the Major built three slave cabins up near their big house for us house slaves. Other slaves stayed down on Clifton Farm after the Bullochs moved to their big house. I lived with Daddy William and several others, but slept most nights in the big house next to

Miss Susan and Miss Georgia's bed on a pallet. They moved into their big house late in 1839. It was a cold winter and more and more snow came. I had read about snow, but nothing made me think it would be so cold. Reading about something is one thing, but feeling it was always a bit different from what you expected.

I remember Miss Susan turned nineteen that year. Miss Susan had suffered a fever a year or so earlier and remained weak. Poor beautiful thing. She was so lovely and refined, but could barely walk across a room for several years. Everyone called Miss Georgia *Daisy*. Oh, could she make you laugh. She drew beautiful pictures, could sew better than anyone I ever knew, and sang like an angel. I remember, brings tears to my ol' eyes remembering Miss Daisy.

Daddy William and I was happy living in Roswell. But we still saved for to buy our freedom. Never once did we forget what we really wanted. Now there wasn't any free coloreds in Roswell. Only, lots of white folks and lots of slaves. Master Barrington King and Mister John Dunwoody and others had lots of slaves. Mister King, he was a tough man. Kindly to his neighbors and friends, but didn't hold with his field slaves not working hard.

The Year 1841

I remember 1841 for many, many reasons. I had lived twenty-one years by then. I lived in slavery, still seeking my freedom. Daddy William and me, well, we still saved our money. And, I fell in love for the first time ever. Now don't you get me wrong, I had been sweet on many a boy before that year. But that time, well, that time it was love, pure and simple love.

I still worked in the workshop most days, but I would walk down to the town square with Miss Daisy and she would go into the mill store and post her letters. Miss Daisy wrote lots of letters to family and friends back in Savannah and even up North. Mistress Martha did not want Miss Daisy walking alone so, one of us always accompanied her. I learned that big word from Mistress Martha.

"Leah, accompany Miss Georgia to the post, then get yourself off to the workshop" she would say most mornings.

Meant we would walk along, talking mostly like friends, not slave and master. We would talk about the weather, flowers, birds we spotted, and how things were in the slave cabins and the big houses. On just such a walk, accompanying Miss Daisy, I met Stephen.

Now Mister Camp, at the mill store, never did like coloreds coming in unless we had business for our masters. The mill owned the store, and Mister Camp, a Northern man, ran it most days. He didn't consider being Miss Daisy's companion as business, so I would stop off across the little dirt lane what went all the way around the town square and sit on the grass and wait for Miss Daisy. Summer had turned hot early, and as I sat whittling at a bit of wood, a wagon pulled up in front of the store. Three boys jumped from the back of the wagon. I knew the driver and two of the boys to be part of the Rucker family from out Lebanon way. The other was Stephen.

Oh, now Stephen stood tall and proud, a nice looking young man. Some might have called him beautiful. He had light yellow-brown skin and dark, curly hair cropped close. Above his lip lay the beginning of a small mustache, and his eyes, as black as a moonless night, shone under eyelashes at least an inch long. He had full lips and white straight teeth. Oh, and he was tall, I remember him being well over six feet tall. But most important I remember his laugh. Stephen did love to laugh.

I watched as he walked over and sank in one slow, graceful move into the grass beside me. Made himself comfortable before he spoke, he did. Looked around admiring the view, he did.

"I be Stephen. I never seed a girl whittle before."

"I'm Leah. I'm not be a girl. I'm a woman. I do lots of things you might never have seen a *girl* do before.

"Yeah, like what can you do?" Stephen asked.

"Oh, I can make furniture. I helped build a big house. I even carve birds and animals, and such. I work in Major Bulloch's workshop."

"So you say, I never heard of no colored *woman* working that way. You joshing me?"

"Miss Daisy Bulloch be back any minute and you can ask her. She'll tell you." I replied haughtily.

Stephen sat there and watched me whittle. I kept wondering what was taking Miss Daisy so long. Finally, I asked quietly, almost whispering, "You live near here?"

"Out near Lebanon. 'long to the Ruckers. They nice folks, only a few of us coloreds out there. We be in town for some seed Mister Camp holdin' for us."

"I live at the Bulloch's, right down the lane there. I'm waiting on Miss Daisy. She's in the mill store too."

He watched me whittle for a while. I didn't know what to think about Stephen at first. After a while, I reckoned I liked him being nearby. Just when I surmised him watching me was all well and good, the oldest

Rucker boy called for Stephen and off he went, hardly a word of goodbye.

Now, I figured that would be the last I saw of Stephen. But soon, he began to turn up at the square, and at colored gatherings like weddings and funerals. Once in a while, we colored folk would have a pot luck and a dance. Stephen and I became close and by the end of summer we could talk for hours of our dreams of being free. Stephen couldn't read or write, so I read to him from books and the Bible. We went fishing, we danced at socials, we even held hands. Once, when no one was around, we kissed.

Daddy William watched me all summer and had Maum Charlotte talk to me about boys and what could happen. I already knew all about relations between a man and a woman, having read a good number of books. Also, there's not much privacy in those little cabins, so I had a pretty good idea of how married folks carried on.

Then one morning, Maum Grace called out, "Daddy William, the Mistress say for you to ride to Marietta for the doctor. Master Charles be ill." While Daddy William fastened the horse to the gig, I ran toward the big house. Today, I would be needed.

Now Marietta, it lay many miles away and going for a doctor took William all morning and 'twas almost dark when he returned. Alone. Marietta's only doctor was not at home and could not be found. All through the day, we bathed little Charles with cool cloths and tried to tempt him with drinks of sweet tea and water. He lay there so still and so hot. Mistress Martha sent all the other children away, while she and Maum Grace kept watch. The Major done walked a path in the hall floor, back and forth, back and forth he walked. I heard him praying and pleading. The next morning little Charles lay dead in his bed.

It seemed the Major and Mistress Bulloch might never stop crying. They held their remaining children tight and forbid them to go out of the house. They didn't forget us colored. No, sir. Mistress Bulloch forbid us from going off from the house and cabins. They kept us close and worried if one of us even seemed a bit sick.

Many, many others fell to the scarlet fever before summer ended. Colored children too. Even a few adults. Children died more often and was mourned the longest.

The Major and Mistress Martha asked Daddy William to build a small coffin. When we finished, we carried him to the graveyard on the hill above the mill and put little Charles in the ground. Major Bulloch ordered a stone with his name and age, only two years and nine months, had it brought all the way from Charleston, he did.

White children who died of the fever were buried in the cemetery on the hill, children from the big houses, and children from the mill settlement. Those colored children what passed that summer, well, we buried them in the forest, like we use to do at Laurel View. Went at night, when the chores be all done. Used torches to light our way, we did. We carried those small thin bodies wrapped in whatever we could find, to the area around the white folks cemetery and dug graves among the trees. One night, we was buryin' a child from one of Master Barrington King's slave families when I heard the talk.

"Seems the fever done hit hard out to Lebanon too. The Hembree family done lost a child, and the Rucker children all be sick with the scarlet fever. Every last one of them children be sick. They done lost two slaves. Both of them done been growed," whispered a man I didn't know to Daddy Luke.

He had not seen me listening and spoke again, "Young Stephen, the one done been talkin' with Leah, they buried him just last evenin'."

Daddy Luke turned and saw me listening. He knew I'd heard. Calling Daddy William over, they walked me back to the cabins and put me to bed. Daddy William later told me he sat there with me for three days and three night before I spoke.

"Daddy, why?"

"The way of death child, can't be explained, simply the way of death. It's just so, just so."

I know 'twas was not a real reason my Stephen was taken. I also know God has his own plans for us all, colored and white. Daddy William and I kept hopin' that freedom be in God's plan like it was in our plans. Seems like God must had a reason for keeping his plans from us.

I never spoke of Stephen again, not till I tell you this story today. Some things simply don't need telling. I guess they's too hard to tell. But I remembered, always.

The Years 1842 to 1848

I remember. Oh, 'bout six years passed.
Summers came and went. Slaves married, white people
married. The colony grew 'cause more and more people
came to work in those mill buildings. I worked in Daddy
William's woodshop most days. Now, some masters
made their slaves marry and have children. Master
Barrington King, he was one of those who did. Not
the Major, no sir, not him. Now, if'en we wanted to
marry he would provide the broomstick and give us extra
rations for a party. Sometimes even a ham.

Now you look a mite puzzled Miss Elliott, you
rightly do. Didn't you know slaves who wished to marry
only jumped over a broomstick while holding hands?
Wasn't no legal ceremony in those days. Now the Major
and Mistress Martha would often as not send for the
preacher to hold a ceremony and say the right words,
but most masters didn't bother.

I had never married, never even thought of it since Stephen died. I watched and even helped with babies being born. Many colored babies came into this world with us friends and family to help out. Why Maum Grace had one every year or so. Poor thing, none of them lived more than a few days. Finally she had one and named it *Comesee*.

Mistress Martha done asked her, "Why'd you name your baby *Comesee*, Maum Grace? It seems like a mighty strange name."

Maum Grace smiled down on the small, black baby girl she held and whispered, "oh, Mistress, she be like all the others just come see the world and go."

Mistress Martha sat and cried with Maum Grace, cooing over her little one. But the Lord, well, He has a sense of humor, for Comesee grew up and had many, many children of her own. I heard she died late last year. Never left Roswell her entire life. At least she died free.

Mistress Martha gave the Major one more son in 1842, sometime in early summer. Named him Irvine Stephens Bulloch. The Major doted on his boy, like he had all the others. Doted on all his children, loved babies. Never seen a man like him. Even had dolls shipped from England for the girls. Had eyes what opened and closed with silk dresses, leather shoes, and even real hair on their china heads.

Master Daniel went off to the Princeton College where his daddy the Senator had studied. We didn't see much of him. When he came home in 1844, he took off for Europe with Mister Hutchison. Now, Master Jimmie had joined the Navy, oh, back in 1839 or so. We didn't see much of him either. Not long after, the Major took all the family to Charleston and then him and Miss Susan and Miss Georgia went off to Europe. They stayed all summer, taking the grand tour they said.

Now I have to say, I was jealous. I had read all the books Miss Susan and Miss Daisy read about Europe. I dreamed of seeing all those castles and palaces. I wanted to see museums and art. I remember crying on Daddy William's shoulder with almost a feeling of grief, knowing I could not go. Instead I saw Roswell, day after day, year after year.

Now by 1848, Miss Daisy was ill with the consumption. Pale as a ghost, could hardly talk without coughing. She died late in the summer. Miss Susan, though still a bit weak, had met a man, funny name, Hilborne West, of Philadelphia. She was 28 years old that year and a wealthy woman. She had all her inherited money from her father the Senator like Daisy and Daniel had. Then, when Daisy died, she done left most of her money to Susan. Now, I don't think Mister Hilborne had much money, but he was educated and head over heels for Miss Susan. Treated her like a princess from one of those fairy tales we read as children. Mistress Martha and the Major approved of the match. Never saw Miss Susan so happy, despite Daisy's passing. They put Miss Daisy right next to little Charles in a stone tomb Mistress Martha ordered from somewhere far off. Came by wagon, it did. I remember Miss Daisy did not want to be put in the ground. No, sir.

Seems like death still hung around all the time. Simply waiting, just so, just so.

The Years
1849
to
1853

Now when I tell you about those next few years, well Miss Elliott, that's most all I can tell you about the family. But I figure I better start with 1849. In January, Miss Susan married Mister West. You see, the family was still mourning Miss Daisy, so it was a quiet wedding, only a few friends and family, right there at the house.

Then everything changed in February. The Major, well, he done died at the Presbyterian Church while teaching Sunday school. Daddy William and I was not at the Presbyterian, but at the little Negro Baptist church when Maum Grace walked right in and whispered the news in Daddy William's ear. Not knowing what was happening, I followed him out. We arrived home and watched as Master Barrington King's wagon drove up to the house with the Major's body. Master Barrington King, Daddy William, Daddy Luke, and Henry carried the Major into the house, right into the library. Henry was still a young man then, but strong as a horse and stubborn as a mule. Mistress Martha said he be'd the most stubborn slave ever born.

Daddy William and I left. Once again, we had a coffin to build.

For once, we did not have to drag out all the mourning clothes as the family was already wearing them. Mistress Martha lay in her big ol' bed with tears soaking her pillow. Mistress Susan and Mister West had to take over making all the arrangements. For two days, someone sat with the body in the library, all day and all night. Then they took him off to lie beside little Charles and Miss Daisy. I remember Miss Mittie and Miss Anna, oh how pitiful. And little Irvine, not quite five years old could not understand, begged for his Daddy. Poor, pitiful child.

Most pitiful of all in my eyes was Daddy William and Daddy Luke. Those two men lost both a master and a friend. William and Luke had never met with anything but kindness from the Major. Never a harsh word. They knew he owned them, yet they loved him like a brother. Just so, just so.

Now you see, everything changed when the Major died. The next year, Miss Anna and Miss Mittie went off to Barnham's Academy in South Carolina. Mistress Susan purchased the Major's Clifton Farm, and Mister Hutchison came often to Roswell. He was a changed man in many ways after Mistress Corinne's death, but he still spoke his mind. He helped Mistress Martha a heap. Bought those girls clothes, and such.

I remember how Mistress Martha never took off her black, stayed in mourning clothes for the rest of her life. But she came back to herself in a few years and became a force of nature once again. Miss Mittie and Miss Anna often went North with Mistress Susan and Mister West, but not Mistress Martha. She stayed mostly to home.

Then in 1853, Miss Mittie's beau came to call in the summer. She had met him in the North. I remember, cause she was in love, and I was in love. Miss Mittie loved Mister Roosevelt from the North, and I loved Andrew. Andrew . . . well Andrew, you see, Miss Elliott, he took my heart with one quiet sentence.

"Leah, just like you see birds in that wood, I can see love in your heart, and I'll help it come out for all to see," he said to me the very day we met. He told me years later he had watched me from a far, and planned on marrying me long before I knew who he was.

And he did. We jumped over a broomstick, days before Miss Mittie married Mister Roosevelt in December. Mistress Martha cried when she sold me to Master Barrington King so's Andrew and I could be together. Daddy William smiled through his tears at my wedding. He was an old man by then with gray in his hair and chin whiskers. But he held one end of the broomstick at my wedding.

Oh, I remember the day he tried to buy me my wedding dress!

"Leah, you cannot be married in that old calico dress. You's got to have something special for your weddin', child."

"Daddy William, you know I don't need a special dress to get married, not like Miss Mittie is havin'."

But he was determined, and we all knew how determined he could be, especially Mistress Martha, so when he started in with in his explanation of why I needed a new dress for my wedding, Mistress Martha turned and opened her wardrobe. Then she handed him a soft blue wool dress and two petticoats she never planned to wear again. Remember Mistress Martha wore only black from the time of the Major's death until death came for her.

I had never worn anything so beautiful. The gown had a full skirt with yards and yards of dark blue trimming in a Greek key pattern and lace at the neck and edges of the sleeves. The bodice needed a bit of altering, but Miss Anna helped me make it over to fit. I stood a bit taller than Mistress Martha, but no one cared if it was a tad short. Daddy William bought me a brand new pair of slippers, soft leather and dyed to match the gown. Miss Anna even dug out some undergarments that had belonged to Miss Daisy. I felt quite like a lady that evening. See slaves, well, they marry at night since day times they had too many chores and such to carry on with. Night times, we were mostly free to do as we wanted. 'Ceptin' if we left our home place, we needed to be sure the Master knew where we was going and why. Mistress Martha trusted us pretty much and rarely did any of us have to report our whereabouts. Now Master Barrington King was a different sort all together. Most of his slaves had to have permission to leave the grounds for any reason at all. I had the most terrible time rememberin' to go ask permission to go gather wood by the riverbank.

Anyway, back to the night, I married Andrew. I proudly married Andrew, me a carpenter, a slave, a colored woman in a dress made for Mistress Martha Stewart Elliott Bulloch. We married in the Major's barn. It was cold that evening and snow began to fall at dusk. But we kept warm by the fires and ate and danced until we could dance no more. Mistress Martha gave us a big ol' smoked ham, and Maum Charlotte baked us sweet potato pies in the house's beehive oven. Colored folks from all over town came by and wished us well. A few people brought gifts like handmade quilts or bits of spices and herbs. Mistress Martha gave me two days all to myself. Not Master King, no sir, Andrew had to work at the mill early the next day.

Soon afterward, Miss Mittie married and went off North with Mister Theodore Roosevelt. Ain't that a funny name, Theodore. No one down here was ever named Theodore, least not among us slaves. Everyone simply called him *Thee*. Miss Anna, Mistress Martha, and Master Irvine stayed in Roswell. They was all that was left at the Major's home. Oh, the slaves were there, of course. I saw Daddy William most days at the workshop. Although I belonged to Master King by then, I worked at the Bulloch's workshop, and Mistress Martha paid Master King for my labor. She also paid me a bit each month. With me marrying Andrew, Daddy William and I now needed to earn enough for three freedoms instead of two. Felt like we would never get enough, that's for sure.

Andrew worked at the mill for Master King doing what needed doing. Andrew was right smart with machinery. We lived in a room in a small plank cabin with another young slave couple in the same room as us. That little cabin stood right next door to Master King's big home. Just so, just so. Our room had one bed and one pallet. Andrew and I shared the pallet. We didn't have a hearth or chimney so our room stayed cold in the winter. Summers, Andrew and I often slept outdoors, being as it was a bit cooler on the ground.

The Years
1854
to
1865

I remember. I do, but I don't' like to tell about those next years. For eleven years, I slaved for Master King. The first year in Mistress Martha's workshop, then Master King sent me first to the house, then to the mills, and then to the fields. Eleven years passed before freedom came. Eleven years more. The hardest years I ever knew. In the big house, Mistress Catherine King kept a quiet, busy home. They had lots of growed children and took in all sorts of men, women, and cousins. Always a bundle of people to cook for, to wash for, to iron for, to set fires for, to tote for . . . Oh, it went on and on from daylight to dusk. I wasn't no good at cooking, so I did all the other chores needin' to be done.

One day, about a year after I started in the house, Master King was sleeping during the afternoon, and I was ironing downstairs in the room off the back. It was hot, and I had to keep the fire going to heat the irons. I had dropped several, and those irons made quite a racket when dropped on the floor. Before I knew what had happened or even heard him come in, he whacked me upside the head with a broom and pushed me out the back door with his foot. I tumbled down the step and cried out. Master King hit me several more times with his broom and then told me never to come back in his house. The next day I was sent to the mill.

Three years, I toiled at the mill. I toted cotton and cloth and water and such day after day up and down that hillside. Over and over, until my back ached and my arms and legs turned to pure muscle. Worst of all, I had no use for my thinking.

When I worked in the workshop, my head kept busy figuring, planning, and knowing what came next. How to cut, how to shape, and how to finish. Then at the house and the mill my head only thought about my next tired step. I tried remembering all those stories I had read from books. I tried to keep my head busy, but after a while my weariness just overcame all good thoughts. I began to hate. I hated my work, I hated my masters, and I hated myself. I became hateful. Hatefulness overcame me. Seemed like no good thoughts ever entered my head.

I won't tell you what I did to get sent from the mill to the fields, but let me tell you my hatefulness caused me to open my mouth and tell Master King something I never should have said. No, sir, we all knew never to speak to the Master in such a way, and that day I done stepped over the line. Those mill workers just stood and stared for a minute or two and then turned right back to their work like they hadn't heard a word. I figured Master King would flog me for such words, but he did something much worse. He sent me to the fields and forbade me to have a whittling knife or to work with any tools other than a hoe or sickle. He also forbade me to have books. 'Twas a punishment worse than anything you can imagine.

During those eleven years, I carried six children to birth, five of them, all boys, survived. Birthed one while I worked in the workshop, one in the big house, two in the mill, and two in the fields. I delivered the last boy right there in Master King's cornfield. Picked up my new babies and walked back to our cabin, handed them to Andrew, and prayed there would be no more. I was worn out, plain tired to the bone. I remember it was 1863. I was 43 years old.

Miss Elliott, I forgot to tell you 'bout some things what happened. Back in 1857, Daddy William passed from this life. Mistress Martha, Miss Anna, and Master Irvine had all moved North. Mistress Susan and Mister Hilborne had left the year before they did, think it was 1855. Mistress Martha done sold most of her slaves, 'ceptin' Daddy William, Daddy Luke, Maum Charlotte, and their daughter. Each day, they walked to one of the other big houses and earned wages for

Mistress Martha. Daddy William did light chores for the Dunwoodys next door at Phoenix Hall, him being too old to do much. Mistress Martha used those wages to pay for food and medicine when we needed it.

Losing Daddy William, well . . . losing Daddy William seemed to bring back all the old memories. The night he died, we walked quietly up past the front of Mistress Martha's big house, 'twas a full moon, and we didn't need torches. Carried his body all the way to the white folks cemetery up on the hill above the mill. There we secretly buried him right next to the Major. Walked home softly singing "I looked over Jordan and what did I see, comin' for to carry me home. . . ." I never shed one tear cause I knew Daddy William finally be free.

Master Barrington King raised hell when he found out where we done buried Daddy William. But since Daddy William be already in the ground, the church folks agreed to just leave him be. I remember I had three boys by then, Isaiah, William, and James.

I mourned for a while, but kept remembering his last words to me, "Little Leah, let me go be with Bess and Isaiah and all those who done gone b'fore. We be free, and we be happy awaiting your comin'. Bring one o' those little birds with you to show your Maum. She'll be so proud." Then he closed his eyes and drifted off to sleep. Never woke again.

To this day, I keep one of my little birds in my dress pocket, in case I'm taken by the Lord unawares. I want to be ready for the day when I see Daddy William and all my family once more in heaven.

Oh, but I done gone on too long about all the sad stuff. You came to ask about my life, and I want to tell you all about Freedom. About Emancipation.

When the war started, three of Master Barrington King's sons done signed up. Mister Daniel Elliott signed up too, but the Confederates done sent him right back home. Had the consumption he did, like his sister Miss Daisy. His wife and children lived right there in Roswell. He died the next year.

I need to tell you a bit about Daniel Stewart Elliott. I always adored him as a child, and remembered a happy, smiling little boy. He grew up to be a tall man, well over six feet tall, wide shoulders, and dark hair. His eyes often looked away, as if he could see things none of us could, and he was quiet most times. He could draw and play music, and even wrote stories for Miss Mittie and Miss Anna. Most times, he was a calm, peaceful man, a good friend to so many, but he did have a temper. He loved and doted on all his sisters and his mother, but dark times would come on Mister Daniel, and those were times to fear. He went off to Europe with Mister Robert Hutchison quite often after he came home from Princeton, and then lived in Savannah for a while. He fell in love at the drop of a hat and courted so many young ladies we couldn't keep count. I always felt Daniel was searching for something, I never knew

what. I don't think he did either. Then, there was a
kind of trouble down in Savannah, and he killed a
man in a duel. Oh, Mistress Martha was beside herself.
Her a good Christian, she couldn't understand how
Daniel could have done such thing. Daniel came home
to Roswell some time a few years later, and you could
see he was troubled. Many of those good Christians
of Roswell shunned him. Only the Dunwoody family
offered him hospitality. Course, they were all cousins.

You know how you can tell when a person is
living with a load of guilt, well, Mister Daniel looked
liked his load of guilt weighted more than a bale of
cotton. Several years later, Andrew and I heard from
Daddy Luke how Mister Daniel had married Miss
Lucinda Sorrel, a girl from down in Savannah. Next
time I saw him, he was a changed man. They had a
little boy, named John for his father, and Mister Daniel
looked contented. I found out he had given up all
drinking. He was already sick with the consumption by
then, but I think he had found peace. Maybe, he had
simply found love. Daniel and Lucy had two children
by the time he died, the second a little girl, named her
Matilda. I know Mistress Lucy and those children had a
tough time during the war.

Two of Master Barrington King's sons died
as well, one only weeks before the Yankees came to
Roswell. Master Barrington King took his family and
all us young slaves to south Georgia to a plantation

he owned. We left Roswell in early June knowing the Yankees was headed south into our part of Georgia. But the Yankees kept coming south.

Now I could read well, and by then Andrew could read a little. We snatched newspapers and read posts when we could. We knew all about Mister Lincoln freeing the slaves. But we kept quiet, 'ceptin' for telling the other coloreds. We could hear the talk and knew we would soon be freed by the Yankees. All my money, all saved for freedom, was gone. As the war got longer and longer, we had less and less to eat. I had the boys to feed and I bought what I could with my savings. I prayed each and every night that those Confederate States would fail. I needed Mister Lincoln to be in charge and to give us our freedom. Andrew and I wanted to go North like so many had before, but we had the boys to protect. So we stayed and worked and planned. Even after Master King done moved us to south Georgia, we had hope. Word was those Yankees were still winning and marching closer and closer.

One day in late 1864, when I went to the big house where Master Barrington King's family was staying, it was empty. All the white people up and left in the night. Didn't take a single one of us. There we were, far from what we knew as home. No food, no master. We be'd alone. Andrew and I had five boys to feed, the last, a set of twins, near on two years old, and I was increasing. I still do believe that's a funny word for carrying a baby, but I guess it was near to being right for I did increase in size, yes I did.

Most of Master Barrington's slaves up and walked off, right then and there. Never did know where they went or what became of them. Only one did I ever see again, she was here in Savannah and many years and years had passed.

Then the Yankees came. Most of us was scared of what was to come, but I found them to be mostly like other white people. Some good and some bad. The good ones gave us what food they could, and the bad ones treated us like dirt. When they left, they stole off a few young men to drive their wagons and carry their loads. They raped some women and carried off others, mostly the young ones. They stole what they could from the houses the white people had left empty.

One young officer shot one man for raping a slave woman. His shot killed that soldier and her too. Bullet went right through his body and into hers. I think she might have been lucky to have died that day. You see, Miss Elliott, things got worse before it got better.

Right now, I need to tell you about myself and how we fared. Once Master Barrington King done snuck off with his family and left us, I realized we were free. Finally, I had my Freedom. I didn't buy my Freedom with money. It might have been given to me by President Lincoln, but I earned it because I stayed alive

through those years. Daddy William never saw Freedom.
Beth and Isaiah never saw Freedom. Stephen never saw
Freedom. I saw Freedom for all of us, and I planned to
enjoy every minute of Freedom. I planned to rejoice in
Freedom. But, well, rejoicing didn't come right off.

I still don't know to this day how we survived the
winter. It was a cold one even there in south Georgia.
Andrew worked where he could and brought home what
food he could find. The boys was stick thin and sickly.
I delivered a tiny baby girl in the very early spring. My
first girl, but she just came to see the world and went off
to heaven. I knew Daddy William would take her in.

When soldiers and others came around the
deserted plantation, we hid. Sometimes for days.
Andrew and I had built a small lean-to in the woods
back of the house and hidden our necessities there
in case we needed to hide. We didn't have any way to
protect ourselves or the boys, so hiding was our only
choice.

When spring finally arrived, Andrew and I
packed up the boys and our few belongings and walked
toward Savannah. Oh, I saw and heard terrible things.
We met slaves who had no learning at all. Never been
no where but on the plantation where they'd been
born an' worked all their lives. Most children had no
family, no shoes, and no food. Many had scars on
their backs from whippings. Colored mothers carried
small children, so starved you could see every bone

in their body. The children too weak to walk, their mothers much the same. Men searched frantically for their wives and children among the straggling line of colored contraband. That's what the Yankees called us, *contraband.* We walked along day after day, leaving the road to hide each time we heard horses or wagons coming.

Andrew and I took two small girls into our family for three days. Then one morning, the youngest took sick with a fever. The Ogeechee River stood nearby, and Andrew and I bathed her all morning trying to keep her cool. By noon, she lay dead in my arms. Her sister, I figured she was about five years old, turned and walked into the river before we even knew what she was doing. Andrew and Isaiah tried to reach her, but she was gone in the flooded, muddy river. We laid her sister's body in the river and allowed her to float away following her sister to heaven. Leastwise, I think it's where the river ended.

Miss Elliott, I never knew the child's name, her nor her sister's. They never spoke. I think those girls had seen terrible, horrible things. I think they may have seen their parents die. While they was with us, not a sound did they make. They ate and drank and walked, holding one of the boy's hands. At night, they had curled together, slept and dreamed, often shaking in what Andrew and I could only see as fear. 'Twas a mercy in many ways.

I hadn't cried in years, yet that day, I plopped down next to our fire and cried. I cried for my daughter, I cried for Daddy William, I cried for Stephen, I cried for those two small black girls. I cried in fear for my own boys. 'Twas the day I also gave up *hate*, cried it right out of myself, I did. I stopped hating Daddy William for dying, and Mistress Martha and her children for moving North and selling me to Master King. I stopped hating Master Barrington King for owning me. I stopped hating my mind for making me wish for more. I found as the tears flowed and poured out of me I had little time and space for hate. I realized I had too much to be thankful for. 'Twas the day I stopped feeling sorry for myself, for being born a slave, and found room for forgiveness and love.

Now Miss Elliott, not one man nor one woman on this good earth brought suffering on themselves. It purely and simply happens. It just happens, 'tis the way of life. Look at Mistress Martha, she done lost two husbands and five children. She ain't hateful, not one hateful bone in her body. Look at Daddy William, and my Stephen, and so many, many others, they never got to be free, but they was never hateful. Even Master Barrington and Mistress Catherine King, they lost two sons in the war. Yes, they did wrong owning people, us slaves, but mostly they been good folks. And Andrew, oh poor, poor man, he put up with my hatefulness for so long. My resentment did neither of us any good. Didn't deserve any of my hate, no he did not. So that day, I gave it up. All of my hate. And once more I began to live. The very next day, I pick up a piece of drift wood and carved my first bird in over six years.

Oh, Miss Elliott, I done tired out from talking. Told you too much. Told you things you didn't ask to hear. Come back tomorrow, and I promise I'll tell you the rest of my story.

Freedom

The next day, Andrew and I gathered up our boys and kept walking.

Along the way, a few folks fell dead from starvation or disease along the road. We didn't even have a shovel to bury them. If the river was nearby, we placed them in the river. White folks walked with us from time to time. Many as pitiful as we was. Just so, just so. Runaway soldiers from both sides stole, raped, and killed along the line of march. On and on we walked. We never made it far any day. The boys tired out from hunger and walking.

One day, about mid day, Andrew and I decided to simply stop walking. We were so tired and hungry. Our boys could not keep up any longer, so we wandered off the road, just us and our boys, into the longleaf pine forest. We made a small camp. We fished in a nearby river for food. We rested.

I guess we lived there several weeks before we found Dr. Stephens, or maybe he found us. Now this Dr. Stephens lived in south Georgia all his life, but had visited Roswell many times. He was a doctor, nice man, some kin of Major Bulloch's. We were fishing when he came out of the woods on his horse. Andrew and I gathered the boys in behind us and prepared to defend them if necessary. But Dr. Stephens recognized me.

"Leah? Are you Leah from Roswell? Is that you girl? Do you still carve those lovely birds?"

"Yes, Dr. Stephens, I be Leah. We don't mean no harm. We's fishing so as to feed our boys," I answered looking him squarely in the eyes just like Daddy William had taught me.

"Introduce me to the boys and your husband, and we'll get you back to the house. No need to stay put here when I got empty cabins need filling."

"No, sir, Dr. Stephens, we be free. We are not going back to be your slaves, no more, not now not never. Mister Lincoln done says we emancipated," I had shouted back even before Andrew could speak. Never knew I could be so forceful till then.

"Oh, Leah, you have no need to fear. I freed my slaves years ago. Don't hold with slavery, really never did. I am offering Christian charity - nothing more and nothing less. I have empty cabins. I have paying work. I have a bit of food to share. Come Leah, bring your family. You can leave when you wish. Anytime you wish."

So we followed Dr. Stephens and was once more beholding to a white man for our food and shelter. I remember.

The Years 1866 to 1870

I remember four years passed. We lived in a clean warm cabin on Dr. Stephens' land. The cabin had a good roof, kept out the rain, even had a wood floor. Andrew and the older boys worked the land. Andrew drove Dr. Stephens when he went on calls at night. 'Twas not safe to be out alone at night, not in those years. I kept house, not in the big house, for us. I taught the boys to read and write. Mistress Stephens loaned me books from her shelves, and I used the dirt in front of the cabin as a slate to teach them their letters until we earned enough money to buy a slate.

There were woodworking tools in Dr. Stephens's barn, and after a while, I asked leave to use them. Soon we had a bed for ourselves with a pine straw mattress. Then a table and chairs. Each day, I set aside time to whittle little animals from bits of wood. I made a pine shelf mantle for the cabin and set each finished piece up there. At times the younger boys played with them and acted the stories I had read them from those borrowed books. I used pictures from books to make Noah's Ark and all the animals I could, two by two, like it says in the Bible. Those were happy years. Our first taste of real freedom.

Those years passed quietly. Our boys grew tall and strong, like their father. Isaiah, turned sixteen in 1870. Not long after he turned sixteen, he left us to go out west. He had read tales of the Buffalo Soldiers, the colored U.S. 10th Cavalry Regiment at Fort Leavenworth, Kansas. So, he used his saved-up money to purchase a train ticket to St. Louis, Missouri, and off our boy went. We got letters for a few years, then they stopped coming. Those Buffalo Soldiers fought the Indians, so we guessed he got killed. We never heard a word from the government, but by then we had moved on from Dr. Stephens' farm. Just so, just so.

The Year 1871

I remember. It was 1871 when I lost Andrew. Seems like all the men in my life died while I still needed them. He was driving the doctor home from a call late one night when the horse spooked and their gig overturned. Dr. Stephens and him was thrown out and both their necks was broken. I don't think he suffered none at all. We buried him and the doctor in the Stephens family cemetery, and the doctor's wife ordered a real tombstone with Andrew's name and death date. We didn't rightly know his birth date. Says "Andrew King, died March 26, 1871, a faithful friend and father." Just so, just so.

Yes, he died on my fifty-first birthday. At least, it was the birth date Daddy William had given me, so many years before. I had five sons left at home, William, then sixteen, was a strapping young man, over six feet tall, smart as a whip. He'd helped Dr. Stephens on his calls for some time by then and was learning to be a doctor for the colored folks. Mistress Stephens, though I never knew her well, paid for William's medical schooling, said the doctor would have wanted him to go. He left later the same year for Philadelphia.

James, only fifteen, he was my middle child. My angel, my heart and soul. So like his father, quiet, hard working. He loved being a farmer, and he was a good one. Mistress Stephens sold him 100 acres for himself only two years later. James married and had a houseful of girl babies. Lived on his land the rest of his life.

Then there were the twins, Luke and Andrew, all of eight years old. My last babies. So much alike those two boys were in some ways and so, so different in others. They worshiped their father. Andrew liked to draw and always carried a pencil, a bit of charcoal, and a scrap of paper. We couldn't afford to buy paper for him, but Dr. Stephens had always had a bit to spare.

Luke was borned different. My last boy has never spoken a word his entire life. He never even made a sound, even as in infant he couldn't cry, made only small squeaking noises. Oh, he could turn red in the face when angry or hungry, simply couldn't cry. As they grew, Andrew always knew what Luke needed. If you found one you found the other. Luke learned to read and write, he could do arithmetic. He's a smart boy. Now Luke couldn't draw like Andrew could. He had a different talent. Surprised us all. One day when the twins were only 'bout seven, Dr. Stephens had called Andrew into the house to hand him paper for his drawings. He had purchased a whole pad of paper just for Andrew.

"Andrew, I saw this paper in town and thought of you. I was looking for a gift for little Ruth and could not find a thing I knew she would like. How about you exchange two of your drawings for this pad of drawing paper, and we'll call it even?" he asked.

"Sir, I don't rightly think it woud be a fair trade. I know that paper cost you good money, and I just draw 'cause I need to. Don't cost me nothing. I don't want to be cheating you," Andrew replied. Now, I had raised my boys to stand up proud and look every person right in the eye, be them black, or white, or even Irish. So Andrew spoke directly to the doctor just like they was equals.

But before Dr. Stephens could answer, the sound of piano music filled the air, beautiful soft sounds like the crying of a breaking heart is how the good doctor later described it. Knowing his wife and his daughter Ruth were not at home, he and Andrew went to investigate. There sat Luke, in the doctor's parlor, at the doctor's piano, playing music, real music. Dr. Stephens told me later he was speechless. He and Andrew just plopped right down on the settee and

listened. He said Luke just kept playing and playing.
He played hymns, lullabies, and even songs we had
often heard Ruth play. She took lessons from a traveling
teacher and played very well.

Quietly, Dr. Stephens sent Andrew to fetch me
and his father. We walked silently back into the house
and found the doctor still listening. Tears ran from his
eyes and down to his collar. Luke was still playing the
doctor's piano. I remember how both Andrews and me
sat amazed and listened to the son I had borned seven
years earlier *finally* make a sound. Sometime later, Luke
realized we were all listening, rose, and bolted for the
door. It was Andrew, his twin, who stopped him. Dr.
Stephens shook his hand and told him to come back
whenever he wanted to play. He did. Oh how he loved to
play. They hung out a little signal flag when Luke was
welcome to come in the house and play the piano. Luke
would play for parties and sometimes just in the evening
for the doctor's family. Mistress Stephens said many
a times she baked and sewed to the sounds of Mozart,
Beethoven and Bach. Ruth taught Luke to read music,
and the doctor even purchased pieces for him to learn. I
had read about Bach and Beethoven many years before
and even heard Master Daniel play their songs. Now
my own son, a colored child born of two slaves, played
Bach.

It was a dark time for me and the boys when
Andrew and the doctor died. All my life, a man had

been responsible for me, first my daddy and the Senator, then Daddy William and the Major, then Andrew and Master King, and then just Andrew. I never felt Dr. Stephens was my protector, but he was my friend. I was 51 years old that year with sons still at home. Mistress Stephens moved on after a while, into Savannah. The farm was sold, 'ceptin' for the part James got. I had nowhere to go. I could have stayed with James, but he'd married and had his own wife to care for him. They needed their peace. Once again, I had little money and a broken heart. Just so, just so.

The Year 1872

In 1872, I loaded Luke and Andrew and our scant belongings into a cart pulled by a mule. I headed back to Savannah, about a two day trip. We arrived near dark, and I had nowhere to go, nowhere to stay, but I remembered the little Negro Baptist church. It was a different preacher who lived just behind the church, but his wife remembered Daddy William and the Elliotts and Bullochs. They gave us shelter and food.

Preacher Butler, his wife, and I stayed up late talking about all the changes in our lives in the past fifty years. Oh, how Savannah had changed. The next day, I had planned to look for work, perhaps as a domestic for one of the wealthy families. Preacher had a different idea. The church had a school for colored children, and the school needed a teacher. They taught eight grades and had forty-nine students all together, not counting my two boys. As part of my pay, I would be given two rooms to live in and twenty dollars a month. I accepted on the spot. Scared as I was, I needed to care for my two boys. I had taught them, so I believed I could teach. Oh, how wrong I was. Teaching your own children ain't nothing like teaching forty-nine children what don't belong to you. Just ain't so.

Miss Elliott, I struggled. Those children ran me ragged every day. Some would be sitting, some would be running, some would be talking, some would be reading, and the older boys would be shooting marbles or playing pranks. Three days, three whole days I struggled. I left there each day, dead tired and ready to give up. After the third day, I went to tell the Preacher I planned to quit.

As I marched up to say my piece, he began, "Leah, I know what you are going to tell me, but before you start talking, are you really ready to tell me how forty-nine children have bettered you? Can you say you have taken control like the Lord would wish you to do? Have you prayed about this?"

There and then, he brought our Lord right into our conversation, just like He belonged there. I started to answer, and just as I opened my mouth, he continued, "Leah, life ain't easy, it's just so. So you need to make it bend to your will. At seven this evening, most of the parents will be here for church service. That's your chance, make them see how important schooling is for their children. If you do, you'll have half the battle won. The Lord will give you courage to deal with the other half. Tomorrow be a teacher, tonight be a warrior, just like Daniel in the lion's den, and you can begin to win the battle."

So I spoke to the parents of those children. I'd practiced all afternoon what I wanted to say. I set down rules for behavior and told how they would be carried out and asked for their cooperation. I spoke personally with the parents of the worst behaved students.

The next morning at eight o'clock when I rang the school bell, I became a teacher. I placed unruly students right up front and made them each responsible for a younger student. I gave extra work for breaking of rules and kept them after class to make up for lost time. I also started reading to them my boys' favorite stories, like those of King Arthur and the Round Table and 1001 Arabian Nights. I would read more if their work was finished and behavior was good. I liked teaching. I stayed three years. I remember.

The Year 1875

I remember. 1875 was the year I wrote to
Mistress Susan. All those years since Emancipation,
I had carried her last letter to us in Roswell, delivered
right before the war started. You see, I needed help.
Luke became ill not long after Christmas. By the
spring, he had lost weight and could barely keep down
any food. I had taken him to doctors in Savannah, but
none could tell us why he suffered like he did. I got
this idea to take Luke north to see William. When he
became a doctor, he settled in Pittsburgh to care for
the colored folks there. I needed three train tickets,
one for me, one for Luke, and one for Andrew. I had
money saved enough for one ticket and our food on the
journey. The church took up a special collection and
gave me money for one more ticket. Now I hated asking

Mistress Susan for money, but I could see my Luke was dying. I could not lose another child.

I took great care writing my letter and when I got to the bottom, I suddenly didn't know how to sign my name. Who was I? Daddy Isaiah and Mama Bess really never had a last name. Daddy William called himself, William Elliott. But I had belonged mostly to the Bullochs. Then I married Andrew who called himself Andrew King. So I signed Leah Elliott Bulloch King. I had rightly as many names as Mistress Martha Stewart Elliott Bulloch! Just so, just so.

It took fourteen days for my letter to reach Philadelphia where I hoped she still lived and for a letter to come back. The letter held three tickets to Philadelphia, not Pittsburgh. See, Mister Hilborne West had become a doctor after he and Mistress Susan went North, and he done specialized in taking care of children. So off we went. I left most of our belongings with the church, took a bit of our clothing, and pockets full of my carvings. Couldn't leave those behind.

The boys and I rode the train for three miserable days. The first day we had food packed by the church people. Afterward, we had to buy most of our food when the train stopped. Few places a colored person could eat a hot meal so we ate cold. Luke ate little, but I did get him to drink buttermilk when I could get it. Each day we spent our time sitting on a hard wood bench, barely room for Andrew and I to hold Luke. The days went on

and on, hot and the air full of soot. At night, we had to
sleep sittin' up or huddle on the floor. At each and every
stop, I sent Andrew to find food, and worried about
him returning before the train pulled out again. Every
moment, I worried about Luke, cradled his body against
mine, and prayed for the train to go faster. Did a heap
of praying on that trip. Just so, just so.

When we arrived in Philadelphia, there stood
Dr. West waiting for us with a carriage. Looked much
as he had those many years ago, 'ceptin' he carried a
bit more weight. He carried Luke himself, placed him
on the seat of the carriage, and helped me up like I was
a lady. Off we went right to his house and his office,
being as it was in his house. Andrew and I gawked like
children at the city. Never had we seen so many people
and so many large, tall buildings. Their house sat on a
crowded street, where one house sat right up against its
neighbor. They had the whole house to themselves if you
didn't count the Irish maids and cook. Mistress Susan
provided us with a room at the back of the house all to
ourselves and see'd to us having a good hot meal and
even clean clothes.

Dr. West examined Luke right then and there,
while Mistress Susan and I talked about all what had
passed during and since the war. I learned Mistress
Mittie had four children and lived in New York. Much
to my sorrow, I heard how Mistress Martha had died
right before the war ended. Master Irvine, now a grown

man, had sailed around the world on the CSS *Alabama*, and Mister Jimmie, well he had a bunch of children, five I do believe, and lived in England near Mister Irvine, who had no children. Mistress Susan didn't ever have children either. Miss Anna had married after the war and lived near Mistress Mittie. I told her about the Bulloch slaves, but she knew much of it, as Daddy Luke wrote her and her sisters about twice a year. He still lived in Roswell with Maum Grace and Maum Charlotte. Of course, she knew all the news of the white families of Roswell as they still wrote letters to each other.

I told her all about my five boys, about my husband Andrew, about living on Dr. Stephens' land. Mistress Susan asked about Dr. Stephens as she had not heard of his death. I told her about Savannah, and my teaching school.

Seemed like hours before Dr. West reappeared. He sat down at the small table in the kitchen where we had been talking and looked me straight in the eye.

"Leah, Luke's condition is serious, but what concerns me most is he does not make a sound, no matter what I ask or how much I prod and probe."

It was his brother who spoke up. "Mama, how'd you forget to tell him Luke never ever spoke not one word? Never one word in his whole life."

Dr. West looked surprised and then relieved as he began to chuckle, "Oh, Andrew, sometimes something you know to be becomes so familiar you forget others don't know it. Now, can you boys communicate in any way?"

"Yes, sir, most the time."

"Well, then come along with me." And off they went.

Mistress Susan and I drank sweet tea and waited. After a while I reached into my pocket and pulled out a small wading bird I had been whittling on the train. As I began to work, I relaxed a bit.

"Leah, I remember now how you used to whittle. Do you have others with you?"

Slowly I emptied my pockets. Mistress Susan examined each and every bird and animal, placing them carefully on the kitchen's oak table top as she finished. When my pockets were emptied, I looked up to see tears running down Mistress Susan's face.

"Leah, you have taken me home. You can't understand how much we, Mittie, Anna, and I have missed our Southern home."

Finally, Dr. West and Andrew came back into the kitchen. The doctor carried Luke and placed him on the bed in our room. He seemed so peaceful I was afraid he had died. Andrew collapsed into a chair beside me, placed his head on the table, and began to bawl like a baby.

"Mama," he sobbed, "Dr. West says he's right sure he can make Luke well again. I thought Luke was dying, and I knew I couldn't go on without him."

"Yes, you could've son, and you would've, just so, just so," I whispered, smoothing back his hair and providing comfort for him and me.

The Years 1876 to 1893

    Luke recovered under Dr. West's care. My son
William came to visit and brought his family. We stayed
a while with the Wests. I let William know where we
was and before he came to visit, I rented two rooms in
a boarding house in the colored part of Philadelphia.
At first, I worked as a domestic for two families, and
the boys went to school. Luke took music lessons paid
for by my William, and Andrew learned painting and
watercolors. Can't remember just which year, but,
the boys went off to Paris to continue their studies.
Both had scholarships from a wealthy Negro business
man there in Philadelphia. Can you imagine, my boys
traveling to Paris to study? Oh, how proud I was. I
believed Isaiah was dead like my Andrew, but William
was a doctor, James a successful farmer, and Luke and

Andrew studying aboard. I knew I was blessed.

About 1880, I began working at a furniture company owned by a colored man. First I kept the books and cleaned. After he learned what I could do, I started making custom furniture for a few of his Negro clients. It paid the bills and was better work than cleaning white people's houses. I made good money those years.

In 1882, Mistress Susan showed two of my little birds to a man who owned a gift shop. He purchased both for $10 each. Mistress Susan gave me the money. All of it, kept not a cent for herself. By the end of 1883, I had sold everything I had carved and had orders for many, many more. Sometimes, I sold to shops, other times at church fairs, and once or twice to museums and art shops. I only had one little bird in my pocket the day I decided to go home to Georgia. Just so, just so, as I might go to heaven at any time.

I needed to see James, and he needed me. As I stepped on the train to go home, I remembered how I had arrived. Broke, with a sick child, and scared. Now I was dressed well, in a new traveling gown with matching hat, fancy underthings that no one ever saw, nice looking shoes, and with my own carpetbag. I had a bit of money, and I had pride. I carried with me a book to read, my Bible, and pictures of William and his family, Luke and Andrew taken in Paris, and even one of Mistress Susan and Dr. Hilborne. I was coming home.

I stopped in Atlanta and took a wagon up to Roswell. I walked around my old home, but found no one I knew. I walked down Mill Street and up to the cemetery. I visited a while with Major Bulloch, Daddy William, Miss Daisy, and little Charles. I stepped into the woods and told all those colored folks about my life. Next day, I rented a wagon and went to see Daddy Luke. He lived on 40 acres east of Roswell what Mistress Susan had purchased for him. Being about 98 years old, Daddy Luke's granddaughter and her children lived with him. It was a small log and plank cabin with a stone fireplace. He had an orchard, a mule, and a beautiful garden. I found him rocking on the porch. Speaking loudly, as he could barely hear, we talked over our lives and decided we had done pretty well for ourselves.

The next morning as I boarded the train again, southward bound, I thought back on where I had come from and where I had been. I remembered.

In Savannah, James met me at the train, and I spent a few years with him and his family of girls at the farm. I whittled and sent off packages to Mistress Susan, who sold them and sent me the money. Daddy Luke passed soon after my visit. I often wondered if they buried him near Major Bulloch like we had Daddy William. Mistress Mittie died in 1884, and Mistress Anna in 1893. Each time, Mistress Susan sent me the word of their passing. Just so.

The Years
1894
to
1903

I remember it was 1894. James, the girls and
I went into Savannah. His oldest was getting married,
and we wanted to purchase her a few nice things. After a
while, I felt myself getting tired, and moved to a bench
alongside one of the squares where coloreds were allowed
to sit. Little Charlotte brought me a cool drink and
proceeded to go back to shopping with her sisters. After
a while I pulled out my whittling and started working on
a small racoon I had promised a friend.

I had sat there a while whittling and napping,
then whittling some more, when a tall, sharp-looking,
well-dressed man, leaned over, looked me straight in the
face and said, "Mama?" It was my Isaiah, my oldest,

after all those years. I sat dumbfounded and as mute as my Luke had ever been.

"I thought I would never find you. Would not have today if you had not been whittlin'," he continued as he knelt in front of me capturing my hands in his. "Oh, Mama, I have seen so much, I have so much to tell you, and I want to hear all about your life, where's Papa? Is he with you? And William and James and the twins? Tell me all."

When I finally found my voice, I kept saying, "We thought you was dead, killed by Indians, we thought you was dead."

"Not hardly," he replied.

It took days and days for James and I to tell Isaiah all what had happened and for him to tell us all his stories about the west, about soldiering, and about searching for us. We talked and cried, then talked some more. I took him to his father's grave. We wrote to Luke and Andrew in Paris and William in Pittsburgh. While Luke and Andrew didn't make it, Charlotte's wedding was the first time I had most of my family together in many years. I remember.

Isaiah has never married, never even considered it. But he and I rented this little house here in Savannah on Elliott Street. Seems like the place we needed to be. I continues to whittle, and Isaiah does odd jobs. We're happy together, mother and son. I get letters from my other boys now and then. Andrew and Luke live in New York City where Andrew makes engravings and Luke plays music in all sorts of places. Andrew married, but he has no children. Luke lives with them. Don't think my youngest boy will ever marry. Just so, just so.

Now, Miss Elliott, I've told you my story. So, I expect you to keep your promise. I want to be remembered. I want to be remembered the way white folks is. I want my story told for generations to read. I want my children, my grandchildren, and all those children and grandchildren of the white people I once slaved for to know who Leah was before Freedom and who she became after Freedom.

I want a tombstone, done told my boys that. Don't have to be no angel or lamb on it—just so it's got my name on it. All my name, Leah Elliott Bulloch King. I done remembered for you, now you let others know my story.

Epilogue

It rained the following day, not a hard rain, but a soft, silky chiffon flowing from lead gray skies. The skies never broke, not even once, to reveal any lightness at all. I worked quietly in my room, only leaving to find hot tea and a buttermilk biscuit or two. I ate them with seedless blackberry jam as I typed Leah's story line by line on my Remington typewriter. The staccato rhythm and constant clank of the return carriage provided a beat for the soft sound of water running across the hotel's tile roof and through the gutters hanging overhead outside my window. Like the rain slipping persistently from the clouds, I heard Leah's words slide constantly, ever so clearly from my mind, out my fingertips, and onto the stark white paper finding a place to come to light, a place to be. To be remembered.

I worked all day, finishing Leah's story shortly before midnight. As her words faded from my hearing, I knew I'd told her story.

On Sunday, the morning dawned clear giving Savannah a bright light, shaded only by the city's many live oaks, each dripping with wet Spanish moss that continued to weep the previous day's tears onto sidewalks and many a passing head. Early, after obtaining a basket from the kitchen, I drove through quiet pathways to Leah's home on Elliott Street. As I stepped from my running automobile to knock at her door, I looked up to see her son James walk down the steps carrying Leah. He placed her carefully in my passenger seat, without a word from either him or her. James's wife followed with a pillow and a soft, many-colored quilt. She placed the first behind Leah's back, then lay the quilt over her legs and pulled it up around her shoulders. Still not a word was spoken.

Leah and I made our way out of town, moving south toward Liberty County. Leah occasionally provided me with directions, though I knew she had traveled this way only once in her life and then as a seven-year-old child going the opposite direction. We passed old homes, a few were once grand mansions, others humble slave cabins, those now crowded with sharecropper families. We passed field after field of sprouting cotton, knee-high corn, and even several of rice, barely flooded with the recent rain. Wagons loaded with church goers progressed about as well as those worshipers who chose to walk alongside the gravel and dirt roads. I moved carefully around each group trying not to spray mud or water upon their Sunday-go-to-meeting clothes. We passed churches surrounded by wagons, horses, children, and the occasional automobile, where men stared and women waved in greeting. Men and women called out for us to join their service to God. However, Leah and I only waved back as I drove her farther and farther south toward Laurel View.

　　We reached the small village of Sunbury where I traded my automobile for a horse and cart I had arranged previously to borrow, rural Liberty County's roads being notoriously treacherous for automobiles. We drank hot tea provided by the liveryman's wife and shared our basket lunch of ham biscuits, sweet potatoes, and fruit. Loaded once again into our conveyance, Leah sat very quietly beside me on her pillow, wrapped in her quilt, like a queen on a throne. I knew the way. I had been here only a week before to obtain permission for our visit. As we approached what had once been Laurel

View Plantation, Leah's eyes seemed to take in every sight, every sound, and even her breathing became deeper as she inhaled the sweet smell of her first home. The day grew warmer, birds chirped and sang. The occasional dog ran along beside our cart, barking and jumping until called home or simply too tired to go on. Our horse proceeded at a gentle trot, never seeming to tire, its tail swatting the constant stream of horseflies just as we swatted the mosquitoes and gnats encountered as we passed through shaded portions of the county's lanes.

It seemed the day moved in circles about us, us being the center of everything, and yet again nothing. I remember thinking how Leah and I provided the meaning of, the purpose for, the day. Nothing else, not one single action carried out by any other person in the entire world, mattered. Only our journey would be remembered. Only Leah's journey really. I existed simply as the driver.

Finally, we reached what had once been John Elliott's Laurel View Plantation. As I drove up the rut-lined soft dirt drive, winding gently between rows of live oaks, toward the few remaining slave cabins, no one ventured out to surmise our purpose. No one watched our progress. The Elliott home, long ago burned, remained only as a ruin. I never learned when it burned, during the War, before, after, it did not matter. Beside and slightly behind the house stood one small plank cabin, separate from the others, slightly smaller, its roof collapsing, its door missing, looking somehow lonesome. As I pulled to a stop, Leah, the same Leah who had been carried to my car, pushed her quilt aside and stepped quickly to the ground, using her cane only for balance. Before I could even move to tie the horse, she stood on the rock stoop of that little cabin, holding tight to the jams, looking into the darkness as if seeing someone. I let her be.

I watched as Leah moved carefully around the main house ruin and around the cabin where once her family had lived. She occasionally picked a leaf from a shrub, bringing it gently to her nose, before placing it into the pocket of her flowered apron. At other times, she turned in a circle, taking in every direction, placing it into her memory; or maybe, remembering how it had been. This was Leah's time. I watched, I walked, I surveyed what had been and tried to see through her eyes. Leah's story of Laurel View had been so succinct I could hear the voices I knew she now heard. I could see the lives of the former slaves playing out across the grounds. I could see seven-year-old Leah, tears streaming down her face. I could see the pain.

Yet Leah did not see what I saw as we lingered at Laurel View. Instead of tears, her face shone in the day's sun with a joy long remembered. I wondered what she saw that I could not. Finally, as the sun had long ago reached its zenith and now slid downward toward the west, I walked toward Leah to remind her we had to return to Savannah. Yet, using a stout branch as a second cane, Leah turned and walked past me toward a grove of longleaf pines, singing softly "I looked over Jordan an' what did I see, comin' fo' to carry me home, a band of angels comin' after me, comin' fo' to carry me home."

Taking her arm and helping her along, I journeyed into the dusk with Leah toward the little cemetery, now forgotten by most everyone. I knew Leah remembered, in spite of never having seen her parent's graves. There among the trees stood several wooden crosses amongst a few mounds of earth, some covered in conch shells or blue and green glass bottles. All seemed neglected, abandoned. Yet, Leah remembered.

For the first time since our arrival, Leah continued her story of Laurel View. Like so many times in the previous weeks, she began slipping into a dialect I'd often heard when she spoke of her first home.

"I's do remember. They buried so many our folks here. In the 1820s, a tornado came funneling through Laurel View. They was ginning and balin' the cotton, my Maum said. She told me of rushin' to the gin house to see if Daddy be hurt only to find him and the black overseer, Daddy Steven, pullin' men from the wreckage. Daddy Steven sent for a doctor from Sunbury to treat those with broken bones and other injuries. Only one died right out that day, but many more passed in days to come. They be buried here. Babies be buried here. Old slaves, no longer able to work. Many so tired and disabled they could no longer even walk. This be our land. Yes, it belonged to the Senator, but it be our land. It held our people. Some day, it'll hol' me."

She stood quietly for a few moments, before finally retracing her steps to the wagon, where she climbed aboard, covered herself with the quilt, and closed her eyes.

Very early two days later as the mist rose from the Savannah River and encased the town in its arms, I packed my belongings into my auto for the next stop on my journey. When I turned back toward the hotel lobby to return my door key, there on the steps stood Isaiah. I knew he could not enter the building, him being a Negro. As he shifted from foot to foot like a small child unsure of how to proceed, I called his name. I expected to see his quiet smile of recognition. Instead he only nodded and walked toward me. Without a word, he handed me a small wooden box and turned to leave.

"Isaiah, what is this?"

"Don't know Miss Elliott, Mama wrote a note saying for me to find a way to get it to you. She passed in her sleep, sometime last night. I gotta' be going, Miss. I was afraid if I waited I'd miss you, but many, many things gotta be done before the funeral and the buryin'. Just so, just so."

I stood there, tears filling my eyes and flowing like the nearby river, down my cheeks making it hard to see as Isaiah walked away. I felt myself collapse onto the hotel steps and reached for the string tying the little box shut. With shaking hands caused by my wracking sobs, I opened its hinged top. Nestled in Spanish moss sat a tiny bird, carved, I knew, from live oak. A slip of paper folded alongside simply read "Let my story fly. Just so, just so."

About this Story and Its Author:

The author of *Leah's Story* is a retired archaeologist, who spent many years researching the South's antebellum slave plantations and the lifeways of their residents. She has read too many books to count written by former enslaved Africans, their masters, and visitors to the South during the antebellum period. The Works Progress Administration Slave Narratives served as one source of background for this story.

Additionally, C.M. Huddleston has authored three nonfiction books about the Bulloch/Elliott family based on their personal letters. The Bulloch/Elliott family members mentioned in this book were real people. Their lives have been heavily documented. However, Leah lives only in the author's imagination. Her life is based solely on years of scholarly research.

The name Leah can be found on many historic slave rolls, as can William, Charlotte, and Luke. These names all appear in listings of Bulloch family slaves. Yet we know very little about these people except for Luke who lived to be well over 100 years old.

The illustrations for this story begin with engravings from *Harper's Monthly Magazine* and *Harper's Weekly*. After Emancipation, you will find period photographs and engravings (Philadelphia). Sources are listed on the following page.

Leah's Story is not meant to be a representation of slavery. It is simply a story created in the mind of an author.

Illustrations:

"Slave Family Outside their Cabin on a Southern Plantation" source unknown

"Slave Cabin on a Rice Plantation" *Harper's Monthly Magazine*, Vol. 19, 1859

"The Broomstick Wedding" *The Story of My Life* by Mary Ashton Rice Livermore, 1897

"Emancipation" *Harper's Weekly*, 24 January 1863, engraving by Thomas Nast

"The Effects of the Proclamation. . ." *Harper's Weekly*, 21 February 1863

Sharecropper's Cabin, photograph, Library of Congress

African-American teacher, photograph, Library of Congress

Independence Hall, Philadelphia 1876, engraving by Theodore Poleni, Library of Congress

Savannah's Negro Quarter, photograph, Library of Congress

Two coastal Georgia photographs by the author

Other Books by C.M. Huddleston

Fiction:
Award-winning, middle-grade time-travel series:
Greg's First Adventure in Time
Greg's Second Adventure in Time
Greg's Third Adventure in Time
Greg's Fourth Adventure in Time
Greg's Fifth Adventure in Time

Winter Wonder (a Christmas/Winter Holiday Anthology)

Fiction for Young Adults and Adults:
*Caintuck Lies Within My Soul: The Jemima Boone
    Story*

History:
Mittie & Thee: An 1853 Roosevelt Romance
*Between the Wedding & the War: The Bulloch/Roosevelt
    Letters 1854-1860*
*Divided Only by Distance & Allegiance:
    The Bulloch/Roosevelt Letters 1861-1865*
James Stephens Bulloch: Aristocratic Southern Gentleman
*Seldom Told Stories: Daddy Luke, Maum Charlotte,
    Maum Grace, and Daddy William of Bulloch Hall*

Georgia's Civilian Conservation Corps
Kentucky's Civilian Conservation Corps
Marshall County (Kentucky)

Follow her at www.cmhuddleston.com   or

www.ingramcontent.com/pod-product-compliance
Lightning Source LLC
Chambersburg PA
CBHW070320140726

47910CB00015B/1541